More EROTIC JAMAICAN TALES

K. Sean Harris

Book Fetish

Cover Design: Lee-Quee & Riley Limited
Typeset & Book layout: Sanya Dockery

Published by: Book Fetish

Printed in China

ISBN 10: 976-610-740-8
ISBN13: 978-976-610-740-6

Sex is an important vitamin (Vitamin S).
Ensure that you take at least one a day.

Anonymous

CONTENTS

SMOKING MIRRORS

*J*asmine Crawford examined her naked form in the full-length mirror in her bathroom. *I've still got it* she thought. She held her breasts and lightly massaged them. They were still full and luscious. Her stomach, though not exactly a washboard, was still relatively flat. She turned sideways. Yep, her ass was still perky. So she couldn't understand why her husband of five years was no longer paying her any attention. Their sex life had taken a nosedive over the past four months. She was lucky if they'd had sex four times over that period.

He had brushed off her concerns and desires, saying that she was exaggerating and being unreasonable for not understanding that with his promotion to branch manager, he had a lot more responsibilities and longer hours. Jasmine sighed. Even if that was the sole reason, the fact that he seemed unaffected by the drastic change in their sex life was in itself telling. He didn't give a shit about her sexual needs anymore.

Jasmine went into the bedroom and rummaged through her top drawer. She slipped on a pair of grey cotton panties and a white tank top, and went into the room that served as an office. She sat down at the desk and turned on the computer. She hummed as she waited for it to boot. Her husband had called just before she got in the shower to say that he'd be working late. Again. Fourth time this week. She typed in her password and logged on to the internet.

Jasmine checked her email. There was a lot of spam. Two corny jokes her co-worker, Garth, had sent her and a message from her best friend Keva.

Keva had sent her a link for an adult internet dating site. She had confided to Keva about the problems she'd been having with Marcus, her husband. Keva felt certain that Marcus was cheating and that she should do her own thing too instead of sitting home night after night, horny and miserable. Keva had told her to find a young stud to service her since Marcus wasn't interested in taking care of business at home. Jasmine had told her that wasn't her style; she would talk to Marcus again and try to resolve the issue. The last discussion had been a dismal failure. Marcus had cursed her out, calling her selfish and non-ambitious. He had told her that if she didn't sit all day thinking about sex she might be able to get a better job. Ever since he had gotten his promotion, he had become very condescending towards her. All of a sudden being a bank teller was something to be ashamed of.

Her mother never liked him. Too pretentious, she had always said.

Jasmine clicked on the link. The site was attractively laid out and best of all, free. *What the hell*, Jasmine said to herself, *let me sign up and check this thing out*. It prompted her for a user name. *Hmmm*, Jasmine was stumped. *What should I use*, she pondered.

She typed *Islandgirl*. Shit, someone was already using that.

Jade34. Accepted. Good. She filled in the rest of the information sparingly, not wanting to divulge too much about herself. Then at the end they prompted her to describe what she was seeking. Jasmine thought for a minute. Then she typed: *Hot woman seeks younger man for discreet relationship*. She clicked the submit button.

She was now a member. Feeling naughty but excited, Jasmine scrolled through the members' gallery. Some of the ad titles were hilarious while others were downright nasty.

Stiff cocky bwoy seeks tight pussy gal.

Looking a fat pussy to suck.

Sexy butch seeks hot girl for relationship.

Lonely Mature woman seeks distinguished mature males for companionship.

Big clit housewife looking to trade in the mop for a cock.
Voluptuous woman seeking big dick men.
Couple seeking attractive girl for threesome.

Wow, Jasmine was blown away. She had no idea Jamaican people were so freaky. Some of the members were from overseas but a lot of them were from different parishes in Jamaica. She continued to scroll through, occasionally stopping to read some of the profiles. She clicked on *Luv2fuc*'s profile. If that picture he had in the profile was really a photo of his dick, he was extremely blessed. It wasn't very thick, but it was really long and full of vine-looking veins. It had to be at least ten inches. She read his profile: *I'm an attractive fun loving guy who loves to have fun. I'm open-minded in the bedroom and I aim to please. I date any age but I prefer women over thirty.*

Ps: Yes, that dick is really mine.

Jasmine chuckled. Interesting. She felt nervous as she clicked on the reply to this ad button. *Ok, what do I write?* She typed:

Hi there,

I read your profile and found it quite interesting. I would like to get to know you. Drop me a line sometime.

Jasmine clicked the send button. *I wonder if he'll respond* she thought. She spent the next hour exploring the site some more. She got three responses to her ad but none from *Luv2fuc*. *He must be busy doing what he loves to do,* Jasmine thought. Two of the emails were from men while the third was from a bi-sexual girl who wanted to *suck her pussy until she fainted*. You don't say, Jasmine thought. These people are something else. She checked the time. It was ten p.m. Jasmine logged off and turned off the computer. She went into the guest room where the ironing was done, and ironed a white blouse to wear with jeans the next day. The bank allowed them to dress down on Fridays.

Marcus got home at eleven. He undressed, showered and climbed into bed.

"Jas, are you sleeping?" he asked.

Jasmine was shocked. *Isn't this something, my husband wants to have sex with his wife,* Jasmine mused. "No, I'm awake."

"I'm going to Negril on a retreat with the other managers. We're leaving tomorrow night and returning on Sunday."

With that said; he pulled the covers over his head and went right to sleep.

Jasmine felt like slapping him. *You self-centered asshole,* she fumed. She turned her back to him and hoped *Luv2fuc* responded to her ad. This pussy was currently up for grabs.

Michael got home at twelve that night. He had been playing pool with two of his friends at their regular hangout spot in Half-Way-Tree. Two of his female 'friends' had called wanting to see him but he wasn't in the mood for either of them. It was time for someone new. He grabbed a beer from out the fridge and turned on his computer. He logged into the dating site and checked his inbox. As usual, it was full. Putting a photo of his exceptional dick on the site had netted quite a few women over the past nine months. One of the messages was from a Jade34. Hmm, she must be new. He clicked on her profile before reading her message. He noted that she gave limited information about herself. She sounded promising though: 34, petite, easy to look at, married but seeking.

He then read her message. He liked her vibe. He clicked the reply button and typed:

Hi Jade34,

I read your profile and I'm interested in getting to know you as well. I noticed that you kept your personal information to a minimum which is good. I'm intrigued. I'm also very discreet and a really nice guy, so have no fear, let's get it popping. I don't normally do this so soon but here's my cell # 122-3421. Name's Michael. Looking forward to hearing from you soon.

Ps: Are you sure you can handle the ride?

Michael logged off and went to bed. He was a gym instructor at Fitness Freaks, and he was on the first shift which started at seven.

Jasmine left her husband reading the newspaper at the kitchen counter and hopped in her Honda Civic coupe. She joined the steady stream of traffic and headed to work in New Kingston.

Marcus sipped his orange juice and folded the newspaper. He reached for the phone and dialed a number.

"Hi baby," he purred when a voice came on the line.

"Hey you, are we all set for the weekend?"

"Yep, pick you up at five."

"Great, see you then."

Marcus hung up the phone and hummed as he made his way to the bathroom. He planned to have a ball this weekend.

Jasmine had a busy morning. It was the end of the month so the bank was packed. She wasn't able to take lunch until two. She met with Keva down the street at a fast food joint. Keva worked on the same street. She was an insurance agent and they had lunch together whenever possible.

"Guess what," Jasmine said before biting in her chicken sandwich.

"Your husband finally gave you some?" Keva asked. They both cracked up at that.

"Nope. I signed up on the site."

"For real!" Keva said excitedly. "You wrote anybody?"

"Yeah. Some guy named *luv2fuc*. Girl, he had a picture of his thing on there. It's longer than a snake!"

Keva laughed so hard, she choked. "Have you heard back from him yet?"

"I don't know. I haven't gotten a chance to check my email all day. The bank was jam-packed," Jasmine replied.

"Ok, well make sure you don't act shy. That site is all about one thing. Hooking up to get your groove on," Keva told her.

"Yeah, I know, some of those ads were off the hook. My *loving* husband is going on a retreat in Negril for the weekend," Jasmine remarked, slurping her soda.

"Is that right…I suppose it's a company retreat, right?" Keva said sarcastically.

"So he claims, but two can play the game," Jasmine proclaimed saucily.

"That's what I like to hear!" Keva gave Jasmine a hi-five.

Jasmine looked at her watch. "Gotta get back to work. I'll call you as soon as I get a chance to check my mail, let you know what's up."

"Ok, talk to you later," Keva replied. Jasmine got up and hurried back to work.

T he bank closed at four p.m. and Jasmine finished checking off in twenty minutes. She logged on to the internet to check her email. She smiled when she saw that she had a message from *Luv2fuc*. Wow, he left a number. His name is Michael. She felt nervous excitement. It just got real. She stored the number in her cell phone. She called Keva.

"He wrote me back and gave me his cell number," she said when Keva came on the line.

"Really! Call him now and talk to him. Invite him to come and hang with us at the after work jam. I'll be with you and it's a public place. Perfect for a first meeting," Keva advised.

"That's a good idea. I'm nervous though…" Jasmine said.

"Jas, call the guy and cut the crap. I'll meet you out front at five. Later." Keva hung up and hurried to finish clearing her desk.

Jasmine logged out without responding to his message. She cleared her throat and dialed Michael's number. He answered on the second ring.

"Hello, Michael here."

"Umm, hi Michael, it's umm, *Jade34* from the site? You gave me your cell number in an e…"

6

"Ah, I was hoping you'd call," Michael interjected smoothly. "So, what's your name…or do I just call you Jade?

"My name is Jasmine," she told him.

"That's a really sexy name, Jasmine," Michael said, turning on the charm.

"Thank you," she replied, loving how her name rolled off his tongue.

"So, what are you up to?"

"Well, my girlfriend and I are going to an after-work jam," Jasmine said.

"Really…which one?" Michael asked.

"At Asylum Nightclub," Jasmine replied, adding, "Actually, I was thinking…it would be a good place for us to meet…if you don't have any plans."

"Sounds good to me, I'll meet you and your friend at the bar upstairs. I'll have on a black shirt. What will you be wearing?"

"Jeans and a white blouse."

"Ok, I'll be there about six. Give me your cell number so we can make contact in case we have trouble spotting each other."

Jasmine gave him the digits and ended the call. She felt excited as she exited the bank to meet Keva down the street.

"Aren't we feeling happy…" Keva teased as Jasmine came up to her with an excited grin on her face.

"Girl, I can't believe I'm meeting another man," Jasmine said to Keva as they walked the short distance to the club.

"Don't start feeling guilty…Marcus is treating you like shit and you deserve to have some fun," Keva replied.

"Yeah…guess you're right….I hope he's cute," Jasmine said, grinning.

"That's the spirit, Jas." They laughed and joined the line at the entrance to the club. Fortunately the line was short as it was still early. If they had gotten there anytime after six, it would've been awhile before they got inside. After-work jam on a Friday at Asylum was always packed.

They headed for the upstairs bar when they entered the club. The DJ was playing some old R&B hits and the early crowd was singing along, eager to forget about work and have some fun.

Jasmine ordered a Banana Daiquiri and Keva bought a Rum & Coke. They stood at the balcony in front of the bar and watched as the club continued to fill up. Jasmine checked her watch. It was now 5.55 p.m. Michael would soon be there. Jasmine started to dance when the DJ started playing Sean Paul's latest single.

"You spot your lover boy yet?" Keva asked over the din of the music.

"Nah…not yet," Jasmine replied. She saw a short guy wearing a black shirt climbing the stairs and she hoped it wasn't him. She didn't like short men.

"Hello, ladies." They both turned their heads. It was Cary. He worked as a bouncer at the club and always flirted with Keva any chance he got.

"Hi Cary," Keva replied, adding as she gave his arm a squeeze, "you seem to be getting bigger each day."

Jasmine waved hi.

Cary chuckled. "I'm coming back for a dance later."

"Sure, I'll be waiting," Keva said and they turned back around to survey the crowd below them.

Michael entered the club at 6:15. He lumbered his six-foot-one-inch frame upstairs. He stopped to say hi to a few people he knew and made his way to the bar. He ordered a Guiness and looked around for anyone fitting Jasmine's description. He took out his cell phone and dialed her number.

Jasmine felt her phone vibrate on her waist and answered the call.

Michael scanned the balcony in front of him and saw a petite, bowlegged woman dressed in a white top and jeans with a phone by her ear. *That must be her* he thought and hung up without saying anything.

He watched as she frowned and put the phone back on her hip. He walked up behind her.

He bent and whispered in her ear. "Hi, Jasmine."

Jasmine's heart skipped a beat as she slowly turned her head. "Michael?"

"Yeah, were you expecting somebody else?" he teased, flashing her his colgate smile.

Jasmine smiled. He is *fine!* she mused as she checked him out. Nice teeth, clean cut, bushy eyebrows, nice features. Well built. Definitely more than she had expected.

"Michael, this is my best friend Keva," Jasmine said.

Keva told him hi and turned her attention to the stage where the regular Friday night MC was getting ready to start the giveaways. First up was the dance contest.

"You look great," Michael told Jasmine, as he looked at her with undisguised lust.

Jasmine blushed under his gaze. There was no doubt as to the kind of thoughts swirling in his head.

"Thanks, I must say…you're really hot, Michael," Jasmine said to him, adding coyly, "You probably have to beat women off you with a stick."

Michael laughed. "I'm surprised your husband let you hang out at clubs without him…isn't he afraid someone will snatch you away?"

"Ha! He probably wouldn't notice that I was missing for at least a week," Jasmine countered.

"Hmmm, sounds like hubby isn't handling his business at home...don't worry sexy, I've got you covered like insurance," Michael cooed.

Jasmine smiled. Michael bought her and Keva another drink, and they watched the activities on stage. The MC was now giving away a basket of goodies to the best dressed couple. The give-aways ended half an hour later and the DJ took over.

Michael held Jasmine from behind and they grooved seductively to the latest dancehalls hits. Cary, the bouncer, shrieked his duties for ten minutes and danced a couple songs with Keva. The moment he left another guy asked her to dance and she accepted.

"What's that poking me in my back?" Jasmine purred to Michael. His erection was raging.

"That's your new toy," Michael whispered in her ear, giving it a light flick of his tongue as he did so.

Jasmine shivered.

"Hmm…can't wait to go to the playground," she responded, turning around to face him.

Michael caressed her ass lightly as they rocked to the beat. "I'm hoping we can go tonight…"

Jasmine thought for a second before responding. Marcus was on his way to Negril and she was sure the bastard wouldn't even call to check up on her. Why should she go home to an empty house and a cold bed while he was in Negril cavorting with God knows who?

"I think that can be arranged…" Jasmine told him with a seductive smile.

"Music to my ears," Michael responded as he lightly caressed her butt.

They continued to dance for another twenty minutes but the sexual tension became too much for them to bear.

"Are you ready?" Michael asked in a strained voice. He wanted to fuck Jasmine so bad he couldn't think straight.

Jasmine nodded and went over to talk to Keva. They conferred for a minute and then Jasmine and Michael exited the club, Michael holding her hand and leading the way.

"My car is a few blocks up in the JCB parking lot," Jasmine told him when they got outside.

"Ok, mine is in the parking lot across the street. We'll get mine first and then pick up yours."

"Ok, that's fine."

They crossed the street and went into the parking lot. Michael led her over to a white Suzuki Vitara and they got in.

"So you work at the Jamaica Commercial Bank?" Michael asked as they headed up the road to retrieve her car.

"Yeah, I'm a teller there," Jasmine replied. "What do you do?"

"I'm a gym instructor at Fitness Freaks," Michael told her.

"Really, I might sign up…I think I need to start a disciplined exercise routine."

Michael grinned. "You look great but I wouldn't mind if you signed up…I'd definitely give you special one on one sessions."

"Is that right…" Jasmine said smiling as they pulled up at the JCB parking lot.

Jasmine got out of the jeep and the security guard opened the gate to let her in. She got in her car and drove behind Michael, who headed back down Knutsford Boulevard. They drove for eight minutes and she followed as Michael pulled into an apartment complex on Ruthven Road.

She parked directly behind his car.

"Nice complex," Jasmine remarked. She had driven past it countless times but had never been inside.

"Yeah, it's ok," Michael replied and led the way to his apartment which was right on the ground floor.

"I've been thinking about moving though," Michael told her as he opened the door to his apartment. "A homosexual moved into the apartment across from mine a few weeks ago and it makes me uncomfortable."

Jasmine laughed. "Are you that homophobic that you would move?"

"Yeah, man, mi can't deal with the battyman thing round mi!" Michael said with conviction. "Enough of that though, make yourself at home. I'll be right back."

Michael left her in the living room and went to use the bathroom. Jasmine sat on the couch and looked around the room. It was definitely a bachelor pad. A small coffee-table with tons of fitness and music magazines on top of it; the requisite TV and DVD player; a CD player with a stack of CDs next to it. The room was a bit messy but clean. Jasmine kicked off her boots as she heard the toilet flush and Michael came back into the room.

He bent over the couch and nuzzled the back of her neck.

"Would you like something to drink?"

"Nah...thanks," Jasmine replied softly as he gently bit her earlobe.

"Not even my saliva..." he asked as he climbed over and kissed her hungrily.

Jasmine returned his kiss in earnest. Their tongues danced as the bottled up desire they were both feeling for the past three hours manifested its self.

Jasmine groaned as Michael lifted her blouse and deftly discarded her bra.

Her luscious breasts tumbled free. Michael stroked and caressed them softly.

"Hmm, these are lovely..." He took her right nipple in his mouth.

"Oh Michael..." Jasmine moaned as he sucked on her breasts like a new born baby. She rubbed his muscular back and wrapped her legs around him as he feasted on her breasts.

Michael then rose and removed her panties and jeans in one motion. Her pussy was clean shaven and slick with her juices. She blushed when Michael pushed her legs back and widely spread her legs, obscenely exposing her pink flesh.

"I hope you taste as sweet as you look..." he said and ran his tongue over her vulva. Jasmine groaned with pleasure as Michael spelt the letters of the alphabet on her protruding clit. She was a mass of quivering flesh by the time he reached Q.

"Jesus...Michael...that...feels...sooo...good...ohhh"

Her cries of passion spurred Michael on and he latched on to her clit and sucked on it like there was no tomorrow.

"Ohhhhh...good God...don't stop...thats it...suck me Michael..."

Jasmine cried out and raked Michael with her nails as she had the most intense orgasm she'd experienced in God knows how long.

"Hmm...ohhhh..." she whimpered as she shook from the spasms still wracking her body.

Michael finally stopped his oral assault on Jasmine's pussy and stood up. She watched him with great anticipation as he quickly took off his clothes. She remembered how long his cock had looked in the picture on the dating site and she was breathless to see it erect.

She wasn't disappointed. Jasmine gasped when his dick sprang free. A real anaconda.

She sat up on the couch and Michael stood in front of her. She stroked his cock slowly, looking at it in awe. She took a tentative lick. She hadn't sucked a dick in over a year. Her husband, Marcus, was nonchalant about getting fellatio so she hadn't been inspired. She ran her tongue along its length. Michael groaned.

Encouraged by his positive reaction she slowly took it in her mouth.

"Yeah baby," Michael said, "show me how badly you want this cock..."

Jasmine managed to get half of it in her mouth. It wasn't thick but it was super long. She jerked it vigorously as she concentrated on the tip.

"Work... it... baby..." Michael moaned as he felt a tingling in his scrotum.

Michael then eased out her mouth and slipped on a condom. He positioned Jasmine face down in the couch and slowly penetrated her from behind. She grimaced as he slid his entire dick inside her. It felt like it went on forever.

C'mon Jas, you can handle this, she told herself and slowly backed her ass up on Michael, meeting his long strokes.

"Ohhh…sweet Jesus…oohhh," Jasmine groaned as Michael picked up his pace.

Her pussy got wetter and wetter by the minute as Michael touched a few spots Jasmine had no idea existed.

Michael held her tightly by the hips and plunged into her pussy like he was mining for gold.

"You like that baby…tell me how much it feels good…" Michael said as he switched to an even higher gear.

"It feels good Michael…so good…you're hurting me so good…" Jasmine moaned.

"Who fucking yuh?" he growled, slapping her perky ass with each hard thrust.

"Ohhh god…" Jasmine wailed.

"Mi say who fucking yuh!" Michael shouted as he felt his climax approaching.

"You…Michael…yes…ohhh…Michael!" Jasmine shouted in response as she completely surrendered to the moment. She felt as if she was having an out of body experience. "Give it to me Michael! Fuck me!"

"Ummph…arghhhhhh," Michael grunted like he was in pain as he pulled out of her and quickly took off the condom, spilling his hot semen all over her upper back.

"Ahhhhh…damn…" Michael said breathlessly. "Jasmine, your husband must be the biggest fool on earth. You're incredible."

Jasmine blushed. "Thanks, Michael…that was really fantastic."

"Let's get you cleaned up before you drip my stuff on the couch," Michael told her and helped her up.

"So…it's your stuff and your couch," Jasmine teased.

Michael laughed and gave her a playful slap on her butt.

They took turns cleaning each other's body in the small shower. When Jasmine rolled his foreskin back and washed his dick, Michael got turned on and fucked her mercilessly against the shower wall. Jasmine felt pleasantly sore as they relaxed on the living room couch in their underwear watching an action flick. Michael had made them hot dogs; they were both ravenous after expending so much energy in their lovemaking.

"Jas, it's been a long time since I've enjoyed someone's company so much," Michael confided.

"Me too, Michael. I feel as though I've known you for a long time. It's incredible that three days ago we didn't even know each other existed," Jasmine replied, thoughtfully.

"I definitely want to keep seeing you, Jas. I know you're married and stuff so it's your call…but I'd like to see you as much as possible."

"My marriage is shit. But I'm still married so we'll have to be discreet…but we'll definitely continue to see each other."

They shared a deep, sensuous kiss as the movie credits rolled.

"Are you spending the night?" Michael asked hopefully.

"Yeah, might as well. My husband is in Negril. I'll have to leave early in the morning though. Tomorrow is my cleaning and errands day."

"Not before I make you breakfast," Michael told her before reclaiming her lips.

Jasmine sighed contentedly as she kissed him. At that moment, she felt happier than she had felt in months.

Keva called Jasmine about eleven – thirty that night. The phone rang without an answer. *Is she really still with him*, Keva said to herself, as she dialed Jasmine's cell number. She answered on the fourth ring.

"Hello."

"Hey there Ms. Thing, yuh not going home tonight?" Keva asked.

"Hey Keva, actually I'm spending the night," she purred contentedly.

"I take it you are having a ball," Keva remarked.

"Girl…I can't even describe how fabulous it's been…" Jasmine told her. "Thanks so much for putting me on to that site."

"Great, have fun…I'll talk to you tomorrow," Keva said and ended the call.

She was furious. *That son-of-a-bitch*, she fumed. Keva had met Michael at his workplace over a month ago, when she had dropped off something for one of her friends. The friend had introduced her to Michael and twenty minutes later, he had given her a quickie in the gym locker room. He had promised to call her but never did, and when she called him, he would tell her that he was busy and would call her back. And now here he was all lovey-dovey with Jasmine who loves to act like she can't mash ants. Yet she was over there taking one of the biggest dicks Keva had ever seen, and loving it. She had been so surprised when she had seen him in the club. But not wanting Jasmine to know what had happened, she had pretended not to know him.

Keva sat on the sofa and flicked through the TV channels. She had never gotten Michael out of her system. Those frenetic twenty minutes in the locker room was the most thrilling sexual episode she had ever experienced. Damn him.

Michael and Jasmine finally went to bed at 1:30 a.m. They were completely spent after having sex three times that night.

Marcus tumbled into his hotel room at 4 a.m. with his lover in tow. They had been out clubbing and drinking excessively. They barely made it to the bed where they instantly fell asleep.

The next morning, Michael nudged Jasmine awake at seven. She smiled when she saw him standing over her with a tray.

Never before had she been served breakfast in bed by a man. Jasmine was touched.

"Oh Michael...thank you...you're such a sweetheart," Jasmine gushed.

"Thank me by eating every drop...then eating me..." Michael said, grinning mischievously.

"Will do," Jasmine promised as she sat up. He had prepared liver, small boiled dumplings and soft green bananas.

"Michael this is delicious!" Jasmine exclaimed sincerely. What can this man not do?

Michael smiled and went to get another tray so that he could join her in bed.

Jasmine didn't end up leaving until ten. After breakfast they had indulged in a long, leisurely session that saw her have a record three orgasms.

After getting home, Jasmine put on a T-shirt and shorts and cleaned the house. Keva called her about an hour after she got home but she told her she would call her back after she had finished cleaning.

Keva called Michael after she got off the phone with Jasmine.

"Hello?"

"Hi Michael, it's Keva."

"Hey, wassup."

"Why you did treat me so bad Michael?"

"Look Keva, don't bother with the foolishness...you know you was the one who came on to me. I didn't mislead you or anything," Michael said, exasperated.

"You promised to call me but you never did," Keva pouted.

"I was trying to be nice Keva but obviously you can't take a hint. Forget my number!" Michael hung up and resumed watching his basketball game. *What the hell is wrong with that slut*, Marcus thought, thoroughly annoyed.

Keva cursed as she heard the dial tone in her ear. *That fucking asshole*, she fumed. *I hope his dick falls off.*

Jasmine finished cleaning the house at 1:30 p.m. She showered and put on a short denim skirt she hadn't worn in ages and a blue baby-T. She slipped on her white Nine West sandals and got in her car. She had a dental appointment at 2:15 and she planned to go lingerie shopping. She wanted to wear something sexy for Michael tonight.

Michael had straightened up the apartment and did two loads of laundry after watching the basketball game. He was outside cleaning his jeep when his cell phone rang. It was Melissa. He had forgotten that she was coming back from Miami today. Melissa was a hot, light-complexioned beauty he had met three weeks ago. She had gone up to Miami to shop and spend a week with her boyfriend.

"Hi Mel," he said pleasantly.

"Hi baby," she gushed. "I came in an hour ago. I bought back something nice for you."

"Mmmm…sounds good. I won't be able to see you until tomorrow evening though babe. I have to go to Mandeville and I won't be back until then."

"Aww Michael! I took the early flight so that I could spend the rest of the day with you!"

That's one of the things I can't take with her enuh man! Michael sighed inwardly, whine too damn much. Aloud he said, "Just relax baby. It's an emergency. I'll make it up to you tomorrow." He didn't want to ruffle her feathers too much. Though he was really feeling Jasmine, Melissa was fun and she definitely knew how to treat a man.

"You'd better…call me later to let me know you got to Mandeville ok."

"No doubt baby, later." Michael hung up the phone and resumed cleaning his vehicle.

Jasmine headed over to Michael's apartment at 5 p.m. She had purchased a sexy little Victoria Secret number from the lingerie shop in the Mall Plaza. She had also bought them Chinese food for dinner. Michael was just getting out of the shower when Jasmine arrived.

"Hi sexy," he said, planting a kiss on her lips.

"Hi hun, I bought us dinner," she responded, handing him the bags.

"Yum, I love Chinese food," Michael said, looking in the bags and placing them on the kitchen counter.

"I see somebody attempted to straighten up today," Jasmine teased, looking around the apartment.

"Yeah, Hurricane Jasmine passed through last night," Michael countered. Jasmine threw a cushion at him.

"Ready to eat?" Michael asked, heading for the food.

"Yeah, sure."

Jasmine turned on the TV and settled on an action movie. She hated chick flicks.

Michael bought the food in the living room and they feasted on sweet & sour chicken, peppered steak and shrimp fried rice while they watched Jet Li and DMX battle it out with some crooks.

After dinner and the movie, they decided to take a walk to Emancipation Park. They chatted about their lives and their families as they watched people jogging or hanging out in the park.

They got back to the apartment at seven. Jasmine instructed Michael to light some candles in the bedroom and wait for her in the bed. Naked.

Michael grinned in anticipation and did as he was told. Jasmine emerged from the bathroom ten minutes later and entered the bedroom walking seductively. The look on Michael's face was priceless. He gasped as he took in Jasmine's lingerie set. It was a sheer, white two piece. It was crotch less and came with white fishnet stockings that stopped at mid-thigh.

Michael's dick rose to the occasion.

Jasmine smiled seductively as she modeled her outfit for his viewing pleasure.

"Come here woman!" Micahel commanded, unable to contain his lust any longer.

"Come and get me," Jasmine purred, as she stood there and playfully stroked her clit. Michael emitted an animal-like grunt and jumped off the bed. He flung Jasmine against the wall and kissed her passionately, lifting up one of her legs around his waist.

She jumped in his arms and his cock probed the entrance of her wet pussy. He slid in easily. With her back partially resting on the wall, Jasmine met him thrust for thrust as he fucked her long and deep with her legs now on his shoulders.

"Oh Michael...you're in so deep...I feel you in my throat...ohh God..."

Michael grunted and lifted her off the wall. He supported her back with his hands and stood in the middle of the bedroom impaling her with all his might.

"Nobody... can't... fuck... me... like... you...baby..."

Michael moved them to the bed and Jasmine stayed on top, riding his cock like a woman possessed.

"Oh God baby...bruck it off babes...yeah..." Michael moaned loudly as Jasmine bounced up and down on his long shaft.

"Wet up my pussy Michael," Jasmine begged, "give me that juice."

Her dirty talk drove Michael wild. He bucked upwards and Jasmine screamed. Michael held her still and drove his dick inside her rapidly.

He grunted incoherently as he shot a heavy load of semen inside Jasmine.

"Michael…my pussy is aching." Jasmine moaned, "I think you hit a bad spot."

"The pain will soon pass baby," Michael said, catching his breath. "If it doesn't, I'll ice it for you."

"That's not funny you barbarian," Jasmine said, slapping him on his arm.

Michael grinned and kissed her. After a few minutes, they got up and went to the living room where they watched the championship bout between Antonio Tarver and Roy Jones Jr. on HBO. Michael woke up at 2:30 on the couch and realized they'd fallen sleep watching TV. He didn't even know who had won the fight. He turned the TV off and lifted Jasmine to the bedroom. She was dead to the world.

The following morning, Jasmine was again treated to breakfast in bed. This time Michael made ackee & saltfish and fried dumplings. After breakfast, Michael went and got the newspaper. They lazed around and played board games for most of the morning. Jasmine couldn't tell the last time she had enjoyed a weekend so much.

Marcus checked the time as he entered Washington Boulevard. His lover was next to him bobbing to the hip hop music playing on the CD. *Ah, these youngsters*, Marcus thought, *they don't have a clue what good music is.* They had left Negril at nine-thirty. Marcus wanted to get back to Kingston in time to play golf with the senior management of the company. They met for golf every Sunday at the Trafalgar Club and he had been invited. It was now 1:30 p.m. Fortunately his hangover from last night was almost non-existent courtesy of a concoction given to him by one of the waiters at the hotel.

Jasmine got up at 1:30 and went to use the bathroom. It was time to go home.

"Baby, I need to get going," she said to Michael when she came back into the living room, fully dressed.

He hugged and kissed her. "I had a really good time this weekend Jas."

"Me too baby…me too."

Marcus pulled into the apartment complex and they exited the vehicle. *Isn't that Jasmine's car* he thought, as he passed the blue Honda Civic Coupe. He was about to check the license plate number when his lover pinched him hard on his ass and ran inside. Marcus yelped and gave chase.

Michael heard the commotion in the hallway. "Sounds like my homo neighbour is back," he said distastefully. He opened the door and Jasmine followed.

Jasmine dropped her duffel bag in shock as she stared in disgust at the two men kissing by the door to the other apartment.

"Jesus Christ…Marcus!" Jasmine said in a loud whisper.

GOLD DIGGER

*S*asha Arnold checked her appearance in the mirror once more before heading out to the living room. She looked fabulous. Her silky, shoulder length mane was shiny and lustrous courtesy of an earlier trip to the hair salon. Her make-up was flawless and a lovely black dress which showed off quite a bit of chocolate flesh at the back, adorned her five-foot-ten-inch hourglass frame. Her sexy four-inch stilettos and the diamond set her ex-boyfriend had bought her completed the ensemble.

She was going to have dinner at JaJa's – the new ultra-expensive eatery on Montego Bay's hip strip. Audley gaped at her when she entered the living room.

"You look stunning," he told her.

Sasha smiled. Another one bites the dust. "Thank you."

"Kim, I'm off," Sasha said to the closed guest room door. Kim continued reading her magazine and didn't respond.

Kim was her best friend from Kingston who had come to visit for a week. She was peeved that Sasha was going out and leaving her in the house.

Audley stepped out into the hallway and Sasha locked the door behind them.

"So, what are we doing after dinner?" Audley asked as they walked to his car.

"If you play your cards right…each other," Sasha replied saucily as he opened the door for her to get in. Audley's heartbeat accelerated as he got in the car and the large Mercedes sedan pulled off into the busy Saturday night traffic. This young hot filly was certainly a bold one.

Sasha had met Audley Moore at the supermarket earlier that day. She was standing in line at the cashier, looking sexy in a ribbed designer tank top and denim shorts that stopped just below her perky ass, when he pushed his trolley over and came in line behind her.

"Hi there," he had said, extending his hand, "I'm Audley Moore."

She had given him a quick handshake. "I'm Sasha."

"Nice to meet you Sasha." His eyes had roamed lustfully all over her body.

Sasha had ignored him after that and paid her bill and went outside. She was about to get into a cab when he appeared beside her.

"I'll be happy to give you a ride," He had offered. "My Mercedes is parked just over there." He gestured to a large black Benz parked about forty feet away.

Sasha had hesitated for a moment then she nodded. He went and got the car and placed her two bags in the trunk. The sweaty cab driver grumbled under his breath about losing out on his fare. Sasha hopped in and relaxed on the plush leather seat. *Ah, this is what I'm used to,* she had thought to herself. Her ex-boyfriend, Chris, was currently in the US serving a twenty year prison sentence. The DEA had raided his New York apartment over a year and a half ago and found fifteen kilos of cocaine and a large quantity of compressed ganja. He had gotten a steep sentence for possession of and intent to distribute illegal drugs. Sasha had only visited him in jail once. He had written numerous letters to her but had stopped after a while when he realized that Sasha had no intention of keeping in touch with him. She got to keep the apartment and the BMW X5 that he had owned in Jamaica. She needed a new man as the X5 was in the shop and she couldn't afford to fix it. She was also running out of money and she had recently dumped the recording artiste she had been dating. He had started complaining that Sasha was too expensive to maintain.

Cheap ass, Sasha had fumed. The man had three top ten singles and was griping about paying for a shopping trip to New York.

Getting a job was out of the question. Sasha had never worked a day in her life.

"So, where do you live?" Audley had asked, his eyes lingering on her long, toned legs instead of watching the road.

"At the apartment complex in Cornwall Gardens." Sasha appraised him. He was light-skinned, tall and several pounds overweight. He was also going bald. Not bad-looking in the face and had a nice smile. Definitely not my type, Sasha had mused, she liked them young, rich and thuggish; but if his money was long, that's all that really mattered. She could always find a cute roughneck to keep on the side.

He made small talk until they turned onto her road and pulled up at her apartment. He hopped out and took her bags to the door.

"So, can I take you out to dinner tonight?" he had asked as they stood by her door.

"Sure, I haven't been to JaJa's yet," Sasha had replied. "Pick me up at seven."

"Great, see you then."

Her friend Kim had arrived from Kingston shortly after she got home. Kim and Sasha had been very close from prep school, and they had kept in touch when Sasha had to move to Montego Bay, though this was her first visit in eight months. Kim worked in the loans section at a commercial bank in Kingston. She had taken a week's vacation and decided to spend it in Montego Bay.

Audley pulled up at the entrance to the restaurant and the valet took his keys. JaJa's was the only restaurant in Montego Bay that provided valet parking. Audley strutted inside like a proud peacock with Sasha on his arm. He knew she was hot, probably the most attractive woman in the restaurant. Audley nodded to a few acquaintances who stared at him enviously as the Maitre d' led them to their table.

They sat down and Sasha allowed him to order for her. Audley ordered jerk lamb loin with guava glaze, black beans and rice, chateau potatoes, banana and mango mousse, and a bottle of red wine. They talked while they waited for the waiter to bring their order.

Audley looked at her steadily. "What you said to me back at your apartment, that if I play my cards right we'll be *doing* each other after dinner, did you mean it?"

Sasha coolly replied, "I did. But don't get it twisted Audley, I might be easy but I'm far from cheap. Before we get to that we need to have an understanding. I can be your pretty little trophy that you can profile with about town, and I can be your sex machine that'll satisfy *any* sexual craving you might have, but you'll be responsible for all my financial needs. And believe me; that will be a pretty penny. Now tell me, Mr. Moore, can you afford me?"

Audley leaned back in his chair. This girl was something else. "Well, Sasha, I own a few successful businesses. I think I can manage." Audley was being modest. He had a net worth of seventy million dollars. He owned a car mart with three locations island-wide, a travel agency, a seaside villa in Ocho Rios that he rented out to tourists and he was a lawyer by profession.

"So where's the wife?"

Audley paused before answering. The waiter had returned with their meal.

"She's currently off the island for two weeks. She's visiting her relatives in Long Island," he replied when the waiter had left.

The food was delicious and the crowd was the crème la crème of Montego Bay high society. The Mayor, some major players in the tourist industry, a popular recording artiste, models and a Supreme Court Judge, were some of the faces spotted.

Sasha decided if things went as planned, she would dine here at least once a week. With or without Audley.

"It wouldn't make a difference if she was here anyway. I'm sure my wife knows about my indiscretions; she's an astute woman. As long as I don't subject her to any crap, she pretty much turns a blind eye."

"How nice," Sasha said sarcastically. It's a man's world; especially when he had money.

"Tell me a bit about yourself, Sasha," Audley said taking a sip of his wine.

"Well, let's see…I'm twenty-four, no kids and I'm from Kingston. My family moved to Montego Bay when I was fourteen." She sipped some wine and continued. "We were well off financially until my dad damn near lost everything in the financial sector meltdown in the mid-nineties."

"Yeah, a lot of people were hurt by that," Audley said, nodding his head as if he too had been affected.

Sasha grew pensive as she reflected on the past. When her dad had lost all of his money, her parents divorced and her dad moved away to the US. Her mother became an alcoholic and wasn't treating her well, so Sasha was sent to Montego Bay to stay with her grandmother. Living with her strict, old fashioned grandmother had been hell for Sasha. Growing up she was used to having her own way and adjusting to the tight rein her grandmother kept her on wasn't easy. At fifteen Sasha's body was akin to that of a twenty-five year-old woman and she was very pretty. Grown men showered her with attention whenever they saw her on the street. When she realized that men would do anything to get in her pants, Sasha decided from that point on to only date with men who had money. Her first had been the Chairman of the School Board. Sasha had allowed him to take her virginity and when she turned sixteen, five months later, he set her up in an apartment after her high school graduation. She stayed with him for a year before moving on to a young drug dealer who she stayed with for three years before dumping him for another drug dealer who had more money. She had stayed with Chris for four years until he went to jail.

"A penny for your thoughts…" Audley said.

"Huh? Oh…I'm sorry," Sasha apologized. "My mind wandered for a second there."

For the next thirty minutes Audley had Sasha in stitches as he regaled her with amusing anecdotes about his ill-advised and short-lived foray into politics.

"You enjoyed dinner?" Audley asked as he signaled for the cheque.

"Yes, immensely." Sasha excused herself and went to the ladies' room to freshen up. She smiled inwardly at the lustful glances the men she passed threw her way as she made her way to the bathroom.

Sasha was feeling mellow as she reapplied her lip gloss. Audley was good company. That was an unexpected bonus. If it turned out he was good in bed that would be the icing on the cake.

One of Audley's business associates stopped by the table to say hi on his way out.

"Bwoy, Audley, you can't manage that man," he teased, referring to Sasha, "you need to pass her on to a real man!"

They both laughed and the man left after vowing to catch up with him over drinks later that week.

Audley stood up when Sasha returned to the table.

"Ready, Princess?"

Sasha chuckled and they exited the restaurant. The valet brought the car around and they got in. Audley put the windows down, opened the moon roof and put on some slow jams.

"Oohh, that's my jam," Sasha cooed, when Marvin Gaye's hit song 'Between the Sheets' came on.

"Didn't figure you for someone who likes oldies," Audley remarked. "You're full of surprises Princess."

"You have no idea…" Sasha said softly, "Is that my new name?"

"Yeah…you don't mind do you?"

"Well, as long as I'm treated like a princess it's all good."

Audley grinned as they pulled up in front of her apartment. He parked and they got out of the vehicle. Kim was watching a movie on DVD when they entered the living room.

"Hey, girl," Sasha said, "You guys met earlier."

"Hi," Kim said to both of them. From the moment she saw Audley earlier that evening when he came to pick Sasha up for dinner, she knew he was rich. Besides, that's the only way he could've gotten a date with Sasha, old as he is. Sasha liked cute, young thugs who would fuck her like she owed them money.

"What are you watching?" Sasha asked, as she beckoned for Audley to follow her to the bedroom.

"The Last Don," Kim replied.

"See you later," Sasha said and closed her bedroom door.

Her bedroom, as was the entire apartment, was expensively furnished. There was a queen-size bed, two matching antique bedside tables, plush carpeting and a large walk-in closet that was filled with designer threads. A twenty-five inch flat screen TV was on the wall over the oval shaped mahogany dresser.

"Very nice and cozy," Audley commented as he shrugged off his Hugo Boss blazer and sat on the edge of the bed.

"Thank you," Sasha purred. She turned on the small CD player and the sounds of Lady Saw's new album filled the room. *Fitting background music*, Sasha mused, *cause it's about to get real raunchy up in here.*

She switched on the bedside lamp and kept it low. She then turned off the main light switch and the room was bathed in a soft glow. Sasha then stood in front of Audley who by now was breathing heavily in anticipation of what was to come next.

Sasha swayed seductively to the music as Audley watched transfixed. She slowly removed her dress straps and her full breasts came into view. Audley licked his lips as he looked at her firm breasts and large erect nipples. They were perfect.

Sasha gave him a devilish smile and slid the dress down past her curvy hips. Audley gulped when he saw the outline of her genitalia through the flimsy thong she was wearing. It looked very appealing. He couldn't wait to feel it. To taste it. To explore it. His member grew. His forty-eight year old heart raced as he unbuttoned his shirt.

Sasha turned her back to him and removed her thong, bending over as she did so. She held that pose for ten seconds. Audley gulped audibly when he saw nothing but pink gaping through her fleshy, clean-shaven pussy. He prayed he wouldn't come prematurely. He tore off his shirt and started to unbuckle his pants. Sasha stepped out of her panties and turned to face him. She still had on her stilettos. She rubbed her breasts sensuously as she watched him hurriedly shed the remainder of his clothing. *Nice cock*, she thought appreciatively as she closed the distance between them. *Lots of girth.*

She squatted in front of Audley and blew on his genitals while she softly caressed his thighs. She looked up at him and gripped his dick with her slender, manicured fingers. She stroked it gently. Audley moaned. She swallowed his scrotum as she continued to stroke his dick. Audley's knees felt weak. He gripped her hair. She released his balls from her mouth and started to lick them. She felt a bit of pre-cum on her thumb when she ran her finger over the slit. Audley closed his eyes when he felt the head of his dick disappear in her mouth. She got into a rhythm; swallowing more of it as she sucked. Her head bobbed up and down as she increased her tempo.

"Oh…my…God…Princess…that…feels…so…good," Audley breathed through clenched teeth. His knees buckled when Sasha took his entire dick in her mouth, deep-throating it for several seconds. He plopped down on the bed when she removed her mouth.

"Jesus...you're incredible," he said as he sat on the edge of the bed.

Sasha ran her lips along the shaft and took him back in her mouth. She concentrated on the head; pursing her lips and sucking insistently. Audley groaned loudly as sensations he'd never before felt from getting a blowjob overtook his body. Sasha stopped sucking when she felt him getting ready to explode. She squeezed his dick tightly and pressed a solitary finger firmly on a spot about midway between his anus and scrotum.

Audley grunted and his chest heaved as he felt his orgasm retreat. He thought he had been at the point of no return. *Goddamn, this woman is out to kill me*, he thought, watching his cock as it trembled in confusion. He didn't know how much more he could take.

Sasha winked at him. "Not yet Daddy," she purred, "You've got work to do."

She stood up and climbed on top of him on the bed. She crawled over him and positioned her pussy over his face. Then she sat down.

"Ooooh yeah, Daddy," Sasha moaned as she moved her pussy up and down over his mouth. Loud slurping noises competed with the Lady Saw CD as Audley sucked and licked her soaking wet pussy hungrily.

"Suck it Daddy!" Sasha screamed, pinching her nipples as she rode his tongue.

Kim was about to put in another movie in the DVD player when she heard Sasha screaming. She walked over to Sasha's bedroom door and listened.

"That's it Daddy! Don't stop!" she heard Sasha scream loudly.

Kim crouched and looked through the keyhole. The room wasn't very bright but she could see the action on the bed. Sasha was on top of Audley riding the hell out of his face. Audley was stroking his swollen member with one hand while he ate Sasha's pussy. Kim felt her panties getting moist. She slid her hand down her sweatpants and rubbed her pussy as she watched the couple on the bed.

Audley nearly fainted when Sasha sat on his face and clenched his head with her thighs, cutting off his air supply as she climaxed with much fanfare.

He pushed her off his face. "Jesus…" he gasped, "Are you trying to kill me?"

Sasha merely smiled. "Damn Daddy, that tongue of yours felt like a tsunami…oooohhh."

Audley caught his breath, and got up to retrieve a condom from his pants. Sasha licked her lips and massaged her engorged clit as she watched him roll on the condom. *The old boy wasn't bad at all* she thought; *let's see if he can wield that dick as well as he does his tongue.*

Audley pulled Sasha to him and she flung her long legs on his shoulders. He inserted his dick slowly.

"Fuck me Daddy," Sasha implored looking him in the eyes.

Audley grunted as he savoured the feel of Sasha's pussy. It felt so good it was almost as if he wasn't wearing a condom.

"Give it to me hard Daddy," Sasha commanded. "Fuck me like you own this pussy!"

Sweat dripped off Audley's body as he pounded Sasha as hard as he could.

"That's right Daddy," Sasha moaned, "Fuck me…oh yeah…"

By this time, the action in the room had gotten Kim so hot that her sweat pants and panties were now at her ankles. She watched keenly through the keyhole as Audley rammed his dick into Sasha with all his might. *Damn she can take fuck*, Kim thought as she rubbed her clit furiously.

"**Y**es..Daddy…come for me," Sasha said, slapping Audley hard on his ass. "I know you wanna let it go…come for me baby…"

Audley emitted some animal-like grunts as an intense orgasm wracked his six-foot frame to the core.

Sasha raked his back with her long nails as he shot his load.

"Ahhhhhhhhhh," Audley moaned loudly as he continued trembling long after his torrid eruption. He couldn't describe the feeling. If there was a heaven, it was between this girl's legs. Audley slowly withdrew from her and removed the condom.

"I'm gonna go flush this," he said breathlessly and turned to the door.

"Wait…put on something, Kim might still be out in the living room," Sasha told him lazily as she sprawled out on the bed.

"Yeah, you're right," Audley agreed and pulled on his boxer-briefs.

When they had finished, Kim had sunk to the floor as she felt her orgasm approach. She moaned softly when she climaxed.

Audley opened the door and headed to the bathroom. Kim seemed to be asleep on the couch.

Kim kept her eyes tightly shut and pretended to be asleep when she heard Sasha's bedroom door open. Her pussy was still throbbing. The orgasm had felt really good but now she felt for some hard dick. *I'm gonna have a hard time falling asleep tonight* she mused, as she heard the toilet flush.

Audley glanced at Kim again before he went back into the bedroom. She didn't look nearly as good as Sasha but she had a hell of an ass and he loved a huge butt. He would love a threesome with her and Sasha, but even if they would be up for it, he doubted he could manage. Sasha alone was more than a handful.

When he returned to the bedroom, Sasha instructed Audley to lie on his stomach. She retrieved a bottle of scented oil from the bedside table and poured some on his back. Audley sighed contentedly when she started rubbing his shoulders.

"Ahh, that feels great Princess," he drawled. "You're a woman of many talents."

Sasha stroked and rubbed his back skillfully. Audley felt very loose and relaxed. *This girl is something else*, he thought contentedly.

"Baby," Sasha purred, "My truck is in the shop. It needs four new tires and an engine part…I forgot what it's called. "

"Hmmm, how much?"

"Two hundred thousand should cover everything…it's an X5."

She ran her tongue along the small of his back. Audley groaned.

"I'll…ahhh…tell them to go ahead and get everything it needs. I'll give you a cheque to cover it."

"Thank you, Daddy," Sasha breathed as her tongue slivered along his ear.

To his surprise, Audley felt his cock stirring. Normally he would only be able to get it up once for the night. Especially after a torrid session like the one he just had. He turned over and faced Sasha. She licked the inside of his thighs and behind his knees. Audley squirmed in pleasure. He would never have guessed that behind the knees was an erogenous zone. The CD had stopped playing so the sounds coming from the bedroom were more audible. Kim sat up on the sofa in frustration. *Shit, they're going at it again*, she thought. She squeezed her nipple through her baby-T. Kim got up and went back to spy through the keyhole.

She was greeted by the sight of Sasha's glistening vagina gaping in the air. Her ass was high as she was face down between Audley's legs. Whatever she was doing was driving Audley wild. He was whimpering and squirming.

Sasha threw Audley's legs back and ran her tongue along the little bit of real estate between his anus and testicles.

"Jesus… Christ!...uhhhh," Audley squealed as Sasha worked her magic.

Kim couldn't take it anymore. She opened the door and went in.Sasha and Audley looked at Kim in surprise when she entered the bedroom and closed the door behind her.

"Kim…what yuh doing?" Sasha asked.

Kim took off her top in response and stepped out of her sweatpants and panties.

Where by Sasha was leggy and curvy; Kim was short and super thick. Audley's cock lurched.

Sasha chuckled. *Fuck it* she thought. Kim didn't pose a threat; she had Audley wrapped around her little finger. Let Audley enjoy himself. Sasha jumped off the bed, grabbed Kim and kissed her passionately. Kim had never been with a female but Sasha had participated in a threesome before as a birthday gift for one of her ex-boyfriends.

Kim returned Sasha's kiss with equal ardor. Audley stroked his dick as he excitedly watched the action. Sasha lowered her head and sucked Kim's large breasts, squeezing Kim's ample ass as she did so. Kim moaned and caressed Sasha's back. Sasha then got on her knees and sensuously licked Kim's vulva.

"Fuck…Sash…ooohhh," Kim moaned as she spread her legs wider. Audley got off the bed and went behind Kim. He planted kisses all over Kim's neck and back and groped her breasts as Sasha inserted two fingers inside Kim's extremely wet pussy while she sucked on her clit.

"Rass...oh rass..." Kim whimpered as they pleasured her. "Don't stop...lawd...Sasha..."

"Woiiiii..." Kim wailed as she climaxed in Sasha's mouth. "Good God!"

Sasha then rose and directed Audley to lie on his back. He rolled on a condom and did so. Kim got on top of Audley and impaled herself on his rigid shaft.

"Oh yeah..." Audley groaned.

Sasha then stood over Audley with her feet planted on either side of him and allowed Kim to lick her pussy as she slowly rode Audley's dick. Kim licked it tentatively at first, then grabbed Sasha's ass and buried her tongue deep inside her as she just sat on Audley's dick, clenching and unclenching her vaginal muscles.

Audley felt like he was going to pass out. The pleasure was too intense.

Sasha screamed like a maniac as Kim reamed her pussy with her tongue. "That's it Kim...suck me...suck my pussy...ooohhh God!"

Sasha came so hard that her some of her juices dripped onto Audley's chest. She collapsed on Audley and rolled off him. Kim then got to work. She moved up and down on Audley's dick, her large breasts bouncing mightily.

Sasha sucked and nibbled on Audley's chest, treating his nipples to sharp, little bites which drove him crazy.

"Oh my god...I can't take it..." Audley whimpered as the two women inflicted immeasurable pleasure to his body.

Audley suddenly clutched his chest and his body shook as his mouth opened wide in a silent scream while he ejaculated.

"Damn Daddy," Sasha teased, as she looked at Audley's eyes rolling to the back of his head. "No more threesomes for you...I think you enjoyed that a bit too much."

Kim and Sasha shook Audley when they realized he wasn't talking or moving. "Audley! Audley stop playing!" Sasha said nervously. She felt his heart. It wasn't beating. They screamed and scampered off the bed.

"Call an ambulance!" Sasha shrieked, gesturing wildly to the phone.

Kim hurried to the phone, her big breasts bouncing mightily, and dialed 119.

Sasha looked at Audley and prayed that he'd make it.

CIRCUMSTANCES

*A*shley couldn't wait to get home. She was hungry and dead tired. It had been a really long and stressful day. One of those days that made you wonder why you even bothered to get out of bed in the first place. Ashley Peart was a sales representative for a pharmaceutical company. The hours were long and she was only paid on commission. It was a shitty job but jobs were scarce. The Jamaican economy was as stagnant as water in a pond.

She was on her way back to Kingston after visiting pharmacies and shops in St. Elizabeth, Manchester and Clarendon. She had endured a flat tire on the Balacava main road, the manager at one of the pharmacies in Manchester had been very rude to her and her lunch of a chicken patty and orange juice had upset her stomach. Ashley checked the time. It was 7 p.m. She increased her speed and whipped her nine year old Toyota Camry pass a truck that was moving too slow. She needed to get home. Her grandmother was home alone and bed-ridden. It was time for her to eat and take her medication. Ashley's grandmother was eighty-two years old and had recently suffered a stroke.

Ashley navigated around the deep corner on the Inswood main road and cursed when she saw the speed trap ahead. A police officer was pointing a radar gun at her car and signaling her to stop. *Shit*, Ashley thought as she pulled over. She couldn't afford to get a ticket. Getting a ticket these days, what with the increased fines, meant paying a hefty sum and losing points off one's drivers' licence. Ashley had no money to waste on paying fines and if she lost one more point off her licence, it would be suspended for a year. She could not allow that to happen, with her plethora of bills she absolutely couldn't miss a paycheck.

Ashley pulled over and waited for the officer to approach the vehicle.

"Good night, Miss," the officer said when he came over to the car. "Your licence and registration, please."

"Good night, officer," Ashley replied nervously and retrieved the documents from her glove compartment. She handed them to him and took out her purse to get her driver's licence.

"Are you aware that you were doing 85 km in a 30 km zone?" he asked as he checked her papers. Satisfied that they were in order, he handed them back to her and took her driver's licence.

"Officer, I know I was going a little fast…but it's just that I have to get home. My grandmother is sick and…"

"Sorry to hear that Ma'am, but that doesn't mean that you can turn the road into a race track. I'll have to write you a ticket and deduct four points from your licence."

He started to move away and Ashley grabbed his hand.

"Officer please, I beg you, just give me a chance. I can't afford to lose any more points or my licence will be suspended."

Officer Jackson took a good look at the desperate young woman. He hadn't noticed before how attractive she was. Full lips, closely cropped reddish-brown hair that emphasized her cheekbones and complemented her caramel complexion. He stuck his head through the window. His eyes trailed lustfully to her breasts which were straining against the material of her blue short-sleeved shirt that bore the company logo *KSH Pharmaceuticals.*

"What are you willing to do in order for me not to write you this ticket?" he asked, looking directly in her eyes.

Ashley sighed. There was no mistaking what he wanted. Her eyes became misty with tears. She could not believe she was in this predicament.

"Well?" the officer prompted, noticing that his partner was looking at him as if to say what was taking so long.

"Umm…oh God…I'll…I'll do it," Ashley stammered tearfully. "Just please be quick and only if you have a condom."

Officer Jackson grinned and slipped her driver's licence in his top pocket. "Good. I'll keep this until we're through. Lock up the car and follow me."

He walked off and went over to his partner. They conferred and watched as Ashley walked over to them slowly. Both men got even more excited when they realized how voluptuous her body was. Her thighs were thick and her tight black jeans looked as if they had been painted on.

Stay calm Ash, she said to herself. *Let him do his thing quickly and be on your way. Just look at the big picture.*

When she reached them, Officer Jackson led her into the cane fields that lined the side of the road. He seemed to know exactly where he was going. Sure enough, he stopped at a section in the middle that had been stripped of canes. Only grass remained.

He turned to her. "Take off your pants."

Ashley swallowed and took off her boots and removed her pants. She stood there in her panties and shirt with tears flowing freely down her cheeks.

"Take off your draws and sit down on your pants," Officer Jackson said excitedly as he quickly shed his pants and rolled on a condom.

Ashley did as she was told. She closed her eyes and prayed that it wouldn't hurt too much and that he wouldn't last long.

Ashley gasped in surprise when she felt something slick and wet penetrate her pussy instead of something hard. She opened her eyes and raised herself on her elbows. She watched as he spread her legs wider and tongue-fucked her pussy. Unbelievable. Ashley lay back down and looked up at the stars as Officer

Jackson showed her a new meaning of the Jamaica Police Force's mantra "To Protect and Serve".

An involuntary moan escaped her lips as he gently licked the folds of her pussy and inserted his index finger. She clutched the grass as she struggled to not show him that she was beginning to enjoy it. She lost the struggle when he started sucking on her clit. He inserted another finger and worked them in and out of her in a see-saw motion. Her juices flowed. He finger fucked her rapidly as he varied the pressure he was applying to her now engorged clit.

"Ohhhh…lord…yes," Ashley moaned reluctantly as she felt her orgasm building up. She grabbed his head and held on to it tightly as she grinded her pelvis in his mouth. Noisy slurping sounds competed with the sounds of crickets and vehicular traffic.

Ashley groaned as her orgasm announced its arrival by flooding his mouth with her juices. He kept on going until she had to push his head away.

"Yuh pussy taste sweet like honey," Officer Jackson told her as he positioned himself between her legs and inserted his dick.

Ashley looked at his shiny face as he began to thrust in and out of her with slow, long strokes.

"How yuh pussy so tight?" he asked rhetorically as he explored her hot depths. Officer Jackson tried to prolong his climax but Ashley's tight succulent pussy had its own ideas. He grunted loudly and bucked like a bronco as he filled the latex condom with semen.

"Jesus…Christ…" he murmured as he got up off her. "That is the best pussy I've had in years."

Ashley got up and reached for her panties.

"What yuh doing?" Officer Jackson asked. "Mi partner have to get some too. You want him to report me?"

Ashley was stunned. *Oh God, no*, she thought. She sat down with her legs tightly closed and cried as he finished putting on his clothes.

"Him soon come, don't move a muscle," Officer Jackson told her and disappeared through the cane field.

Ashley hollered as she waited for the other officer to show up. Ironically she had been speeding to get home quickly and now she would reach home even later. She looked at her watch. 7:40 p.m. She prayed officer number two was a one minute man.

"How yuh take so long man?" Officer Stone asked when his partner returned. "Ah so it did sweet yuh?"

Jackson grinned at his partner. "Trust mi, de gal pussy tight and sweet!"

They touched fists and Officer Stone quickly made his way into the cane field. Ashley looked up when she heard him approach.

"Ready fi mi?" he asked with a smile and dropped his pants.

Ashley felt like running through the cane fields and leaving her clothes behind when she saw the man's cock. It was huge. The biggest she had ever seen. And it was about to penetrate her. She kept her legs tightly shut as she watched him struggle to roll the condom on.

"Nuh worry yourself babygirl," Officer Stone said as he gestured for her to lie down and open her legs. Ashley reluctantly lay on her back and braced herself for what she was certain would be an extremely painful experience. Each of the six lovers she had had in her twenty-five years – excluding the first cop, and even he had said as much – had marveled at how tight she was; and they all had average size dicks. This man would surely rip her in two.

Officer Stone climbed his heavy frame on top of Ashley and placed the head of his shaft at the entrance of her pussy. He rubbed it up and down her vulva a few times before slowly inserting the head.

Ashley groaned loudly and spread her legs as wide as she could. He rotated his hips slowly, while gently inching himself deeper inside her.

"Hmmm…yuh pussy really tight fi true," he murmured appreciatively. Unable to contain himself any longer, Officer Stone shoved the full length of his long dick into Ashley until he was balls deep.

"Oh my God…noooo!" Ashley cried out as she tried to restrain him by holding on to his hips. He grabbed her hands and held them by her head as he plunged into her with wild abandon.

"Look how yuh thick and round an' ah come gwaan like yuh 'fraid ah big wood," he said as he fucked her mercilessly.

Ashley grunted like a pig with each thrust. Her pussy felt as if someone had lit a match in there. Her cries seemed to excite him as he fucked her even harder. It was as if he was trying to bury her in the cane field with his dick.

Ashley cried for her deceased mother as she begged him to stop or hurry up and climax. After what seemed like an eternity, he finally climaxed with a guttural roar. Ashley pushed him off her when he lingered after his orgasm. She moaned. She felt like she had just been gang-banged by ten men.

"Yuh alright?" he asked in a satisfied tone as she got up gingerly to put on her clothes.

"You and your partner just sexually assaulted me. Of course I'm not alright you moron!" Ashley shouted tearfully.

"Hold on jus' a minute there, yuh had a choice…don't forget that," Officer Stone retorted as he pulled up his pants.

"Fuck you!" Ashley finished putting her clothes on and followed him out of the cane field. *I didn't have a choice*, Ashley sobbed to herself. *I simply cannot lose my licence right now.*

"**A**bout time," Officer Jackson quipped, when his partner returned with Ashley.

Officer Stone chuckled.

"Here you go, Miss," Officer Jackson said, handing Ashley her driver's licence.

Ashley grabbed it and walked away as quickly as her bruised vagina would allow.

"Take it easy on the road and thanks!" Officer Jackson shouted at her retreating back.

Ashley flipped him her middle finger without looking back and got in her car. She started crying again as she started the car. It was now 9 p.m. She should have been home an hour and a half ago. *Those stinking cops,* she fumed. *I hope gunman kill them.*

Ashley finally got home at nine-thirty. She looked in on her grandmother who was fast asleep and went into the kitchen to make her some soup. Fifteen minutes later, she gently nudged her grandmother awake and fed her. Her medication was next and then Ashley tucked her in for the night. She then peeled off her clothes and took a long shower. Her vagina was extremely sore. Ashley ate some left over rice and peas and chicken, and went straight to bed. Dennis, her boyfriend, called her on her cell phone as she curled up under the sheets. She ignored the call and turned the volume down on the phone. He would want to have sex and there was no way she could tell him why they couldn't. Her period was last week so she couldn't use that excuse. She would have to think of something as her body needed at least a week to recover. Ashley finally fell asleep after half an hour of tossing and turning.

Later that night, Officer Jackson, his brother and two of their friends, went over to the poolside at the Eagle Crest Hotel in New Kingston. They had karaoke on a Friday night and a lot of women were always there. They sat at a table close to the bar and Jackson ordered the first round of drinks. They all had a good laugh when he told them about his tryst in the cane field earlier that evening.

Officer Jackson was having a good time, laughing and chatting, when he noticed a woman at the bar staring at him openly. She was wearing a short blue dress which showed off a generous display of firm, smooth thighs. She smiled at him.

"Yuh nah go get that," his brother whispered to him. "Today is definitely your lucky day."

He grinned at his brother and went over to sit on the empty stool next to the woman.

"Hi, I'm Orville," Jackson said to her.

"I'm Andrea," she replied.

"Can I buy you a drink?"

"Sure, I'll have a Martini."

Jackson ordered the drink. "Where are you from Andrea? That's a nice accent."

"I'm from Houston, Texas," she replied as she sipped her drink. "I'm here for a conference. I leave tomorrow."

"Ahhh, that's too bad," Jackson said, "I was hoping we could have some fun together."

"No time like the present," she responded coolly. "I'm staying here at this hotel."

Jackson couldn't believe his good luck. "I'll be right back."

He strutted over to the table and told the guys that if he wasn't back when they were ready to leave, they should go home without him.

"Yes, Mr. Cassanova," his brother teased.

Jackson grinned and walked back over to the woman. "Ready?"

"I was born ready" was the reply.

Jackson chuckled and they made their way to the lobby.

"I hope you're freaky," she said, as they rode the elevator to the fourth floor.

"Yeah, man!" Jackson replied enthusiastically.

"Good."

When they got to her room, she immediately told Jackson to strip. *Damn, she nuh waste time,* Jackson mused as he undressed. Andrea arched her eyebrows when she saw his firearm. "I'm a police officer," Jackson explained.

She sank to her knees and placed his erect dick in her mouth. Jackson groaned and ran his hands through her hair.

"Mmmm…yuh mouth feel hot and nice…suck it…oh yeah…"

She caressed his balls as she sucked his dick sensuously; making eye contact the whole time. That drove Jackson crazy. His erratic breathing and loud moans signaled his approval.

She suddenly stood up and pushed him onto the bed. She then slipped off her dress slowly. Jackson whistled appreciatively when she stood there naked with her legs apart, allowing him to admire her slender but curvy frame.

She climbed on top of him. She bit him on the neck and licked his ear.

"I'm gonna put whipped cream and chocolate syrup all over your body…then lick you clean," she whispered in his ear. "Would you like that?"

"Ohhh yes…" Jackson breathed as his erection lurched.

"But you have to let me tie you up," she said. "It intensifies the pleasure. For both of us."

Jackson was silent for a moment. He didn't like the idea of being tied up but the whipped cream and chocolate syrup sounded too exciting to pass up.

"Alright," he agreed.

Andrea smiled and opened her suitcase. She threw a can of whipped cream and a bottle of chocolate syrup on the bed and took out a pair of padded handcuffs.

Jackson felt a bit nervous but smiled when she cuffed his hands to the headboard. She kissed him passionately and then got up.

"I'll be right back," she told him and went into the bathroom.

She returned a few seconds later wearing a strap-on and an excited expression. Jackson's eyes became saucers as he stared in horror at the sight of the large black dildo strapped to her crotch.

"Whey de bumboclaat yuh ah do woman?" he asked in terror. "Yuh mad? Mi is a police man! Yuh can't ramp wid mi dem way yah!"

Andrea merely smiled in response and climbed onto the bed. She deftly grabbed his feet and restrained his legs as he frantically tried to kick at her.

Officer Jackson's screams could be heard all the way down in the hotel lobby.

THE ADDICT

*V*ctor glanced at his watch. It was almost 11:45. His boss, the miserable Mrs. Tinsley, had left for a meeting and wouldn't know if he took lunch early. He took his pouch off the desk and went to the bathroom. He passed Marsha, one of the receptionists, in the hallway. She smiled inwardly when she observed Victor going into the men's room. He had no idea that Boris, one of their co-workers, had told her that he had caught Victor masturbating in the bathroom on more than one occasion. Marsha wondered where Victor found the energy to masturbate as it was common knowledge that Victor had a lot of women. He was tall and athletic with low curly hair and handsome features. He had slept with three of the eight women who worked for the firm. Except for her, the other four women were over forty and apparently too unattractive for Victor's liking. Victor had tried to put the moves on Marsha on her first day there but she had quickly thwarted his advances by informing him that she was a lesbian. He hadn't believed her until she introduced him to her lover one evening when she came to pick her up from work.

Victor went into the men's room and entered the last stall in a row of four. He closed the door and dropped his pants. He made himself comfortable on the toilet seat and removed a small bottle of lube and some naked pictures he had printed off the internet. Fifteen minutes and two orgasms later, he exited the bathroom and went to lunch.

While lunching at a fast food restaurant a couple blocks from his office, Victor saw Charlene, a sexy half-Chinese marketing executive that he had put the moves on a couple weeks ago. She smiled at him and came over to join him at his table.

"Hello there, Mr. Playboy," she teased as she sat down opposite Victor.

"Hi Charlene, you look better and better every time I see you. Pretty soon I won't be able to control myself," Victor warned over a bite of his chicken sandwich.

Charlene laughed. "Victor please. From what I hear you have your hands full and I need lots of attention."

Victor merely smiled. He knew Charlene liked him and it was just a matter of time before she stopped giving him a hard time. They chatted about the inclement weather that Jamaica had been experiencing for the past week resulting in island wide flooding and other current affairs until it was time for Victor to get back to work.

Charlene was finished as well so they walked together down the street. Her office was further down Knutsford Boulevard. She worked at one of Jamaica's leading cell phone providers.

"On a serious note, I really want to see you Charlene," Victor told her as they stood outside the entrance to the building which housed the offices of the real estate firm he worked for.

"We'll see, Mr. Playboy," Charlene replied, adding, "I just might give you a call one of these days. And if I do, you had better not disappoint." With that she turned and walked off. Victor smiled as he watched her strut down the street. *Damn she's sexy*, he thought, feeling the beginning of an erection. His extension rang as he returned to the office and sat down at his desk. It was Mrs. McNabb. He had recently sold her a two bedroom apartment at a swanky new complex in Jacks Hill.

"Mr. Harvey," she intoned. "How are you?"

"I'm fine, Mrs. McNabb," Victor replied. "Have you settled into your new digs as yet?"

"That's actually the reason for my call," she responded. "I haven't broken the house in yet, if you know what I mean."

"I'm not sure I do, Mrs. McNabb," Victor replied. He knew exactly what she meant but he had to be sure, it was better not to assume.

"Don't be coy, Mr. Harvey, I'm asking you to have sex with me in my new home," she replied coolly.

Victor smiled to himself. He had known that the rich forty-five year old woman had been attracted him from the moment she had visited the office to purchase a home through his firm. He normally didn't go for them that old but the only thing Victor loved more than sex was money. He also didn't have to worry about Mr. McNabb as the two had recently separated, though it was common knowledge that her husband, who was a prominent businessman, was extremely jealous and wasn't taking the separation well.

"I see," Victor replied. "When would you like me to visit?"

"Tonight. I have not gotten laid in two months and frankly I'm in dire need of some sexual stimulation."

"No problem," Victor responded, "What time?"

"7:30 will be fine. I'll have the cook prepare dinner before he leaves. And Victor…"

"Yes, Mrs. McNabb?"

"If you please me immensely it will be to your benefit. I'm a very generous woman."

"That's go…" Victor stopped in mid sentence when she realized she had hung up.

That woman is something else, Victor mused as he pulled the file for a property that a prospective buyer was coming to look at in ten minutes. Christmas was coming and he wouldn't mind a new wardrobe and a set of new low- profile rims for his car. All he had to do was rock her world.

At five-fifteen that evening, Victor saw Roberta, one of his conquests from the office in the underground parking lot. It had been awhile since he had slept with her; too clingy for his liking. But she was looking real hot today in her short navy blue skirt suit and stockings.

"Hi babes," Victor said as he approached her and gave her a hug.

"Hi Victor," Roberta responded. She hated herself for the way she allowed Victor to use her when he felt like it but she was hopelessly in love with him; had been from her first day at the firm eight months ago. She was by her car with one of the rear doors open. When he had approached her she had been putting her files on the back seat.

"You look really hot today," Victor whispered in her ear, causing tremors to run through Roberta's petite five-foot-three-inch frame.

"Thanks…"she murmured as he flicked his tongue on her right ear lobe. She was parked towards the back of the lot and a large SUV provided adequate cover from anyone passing by. Victor had only seen her because he was parked two cars down.

Victor ran his hands up her legs and cupped her ass under her skirt. She could feel his growing manhood pressing insistently against her stomach. Roberta moaned when Victor cupped her mound which was covered by her stockings. She hardly ever wore panties. Victor lowered his head and claimed her lips with a passionate kiss that caused Roberta to groan in his mouth. God she missed him! Victor then whispered for her to go and start the car and turn on the air conditioner. Roberta quickly did as she was told and Victor sat on the passenger seat and reclined it. Roberta slipped off her heels and pulled off her stockings as Victor pulled his pants and boxers to his ankles. He rolled on a condom and Roberta got on top of him and slowly eased herself down on his turgid erection.

"Oh Victor…" she moaned softly as she slowly moved up and down his phallus. It was sweet pain as she had not had sex since the last time he had been with her over nine weeks ago. Victor put his hands in her blouse and squeezed her breasts gently while he urged her to fuck him. Roberta groaned with pleasure and impaled herself all the way down to the base of his cock and started to move in a frenzied, circular motion.

Victor murmured his approval. "That's it baby…wine pon it baby…"

"Mmmmm…I… missed…you…Vic…oh god…" Roberta moaned as she felt her orgasm approaching. She flung her head back and rode Victor as if she wanted to break off his dick inside her. Victor slapped her small heart-shaped ass as she emitted some animal like grunts signaling the arrival of her orgasm. Her pussy bathed his cock with her juices as she stuffed her jacket in her mouth to help muffle her screams. Victor sat still with his dick deeply embedded inside her as he waited for her spasms to subside.

"God…Vic…that was…so intense…I really missed you… baby…"

"Shsssh…" Victor said placing a finger gently to her lips. He didn't want her to get all corny and sentimental on him. He told her to get up and position on the back seat. He then positioned himself between the two front seats and entered her doggystyle. He heard a vehicle close to them start up and exit the parking lot. Victor gave her long slow strokes as Roberta moaned apprecia-tively, slowly rotating her ass in sync with his movements.

"Jesus…that feels so good Vic…you're the best baby…this pussy is yours anytime you want it…Christ…" Roberta moaned as Victor continued to explore her depths at a slow, deliberate pace. He checked his watch. It was now 5:45. He needed to hurry up and go home to clean up for his rendezvous with Mrs. McNabb. Traffic in the evenings was ridiculous going to that side of Kingston and he didn't want to be late. Roberta whimpered as he increased his tempo.

"Oh…Vic…give it to me baby…oh yeah…"

Victor's balls slapped noisily against her thighs as he pounded her in the close confines of the Nissan Sentra.

"Damn… you're so wet…" Victor murmured as he felt a familiar tingle in his scrotum. He was getting ready to erupt. He held on to her shoulders and panted loudly as he filled the con-dom with his seed.

"Oh baby...that was so good..." Roberta gasped as she collapsed on the seat. Victor took off the condom and nastily threw it out the window.

"I've got to get going babes," Victor told her as he fixed his clothes. Roberta remained silent as the euphoria of the much needed sex she just had wore off and the reality of being in love with a bastard like Victor set in. She sighed and straightened her clothes as Victor exited the car promising to call her later.

Victor got into his Honda Integra and drove out of the parking lot without a backward glance. He turned onto Holborn Road and headed to his apartment on Waterloo Road. The traffic was heavy though and a ten minute drive turned into a slow forty minute crawl. He finally got home at twenty minutes to seven. He stripped off his clothes and took a quick shower, dressed in slacks, loafers and a polo shirt, and had a glass of fruit juice and a spoonful of his vitamin tonic. At seven he was back into traffic heading towards Barbican Road. Mrs. McNabb called him at seven thirty-five.

"You are late so I presume you are stuck in that dreadful traffic?"

"Yes, I am. Sorry I'm late...I'll be there in roughly another twenty minutes."

"Ok, but hurry. I simply abhor being kept waiting," she said and hung up.

Victor smiled to himself at her attitude. He could handle her; he was used to dealing with rich people who thought the world revolved them. After all, he used to be one of them until his father had blown the family fortune when he was still in university. The old man had waited until the money was gone before he decided to seek help for his gambling addiction. His mother didn't miss a beat. She quickly divorced his dad and got married to a British guy who could keep her leading the kind of lifestyle to which she was accustomed. She had been living in London for the past two years. His mother had paid for his final year in university, got him an apartment and paid his rent in advance for six months. She also got him a good job with a leading real estate firm through one of her contacts.

Victor turned onto Jacks Hill Road and ten minutes later he was at the gate of the affluent apartment complex where Mrs. McNabb resided. The security guard buzzed him in and he pulled up at apartment 4 and parked behind Mrs. McNabb's Audi A6. He admired the car as he made his way to her door. He pressed the buzzer and she opened the door.

"Again my apologies for being late," Victor said as he stepped inside the exquisitely furnished apartment. Done in earth tones and furnished with beautiful antiques, expensive sculptures and paintings; and plush carpeting, the living room looked like a page out of Home Design magazine.

"Let's eat," Mrs. McNabb responded, and led him to the large mahogany dining table which was set for two. Victor appraised her as he followed her to the table. She was wearing a short, black cocktail dress which clung to her petite figure and five inch stilettos which accentuated her toned, attractive legs. A thin diamond and platinum necklace with the matching bracelet sparkled in the low lighting. Her hair was dyed a light reddish blonde and was cut in a short, cropped style which made her seem younger than her forty-five years. She definitely was at the top of her game.

Victor pulled her chair and she thanked him and sat. The cook had prepared roast beef with mushrooms, parsley potatoes, smoked marlin with cream cheese, buttered string beans and bread pudding served with vanilla sauce. There was a choice of vintage red or white wine.

"The chef is excellent," Victor said appreciatively. The food was delicious.

"Thank you, he used to be the executive chef at one of Kingston's most popular hotels," Mrs. McNabb informed him.

Classical jazz played from unseen surround speakers.

After dinner they retired to the den and sat next to each other on the comfortable beige leather couch. Mrs. McNabb sipped her white wine and kicked off her stilettos. She placed her small feet in Victor's lap.

Victor began to give her a foot massage.

Mrs. McNabb sighed appreciatively.

"This is my favourite room in the house," she murmured to Victor. "It's just so cozy and intimate."

"Yes, it's very nice. As is the entire apartment," Victor responded.

"Mmmm," she moaned softly as Victor deftly massaged the insoles of her feet.

"Wait until you see the bedroom," she said running her tongue around the rim of her glass. "It will blow your mind."

"Can't wait…" Victor whispered as he inched his hands up to her calves.

Mrs. McNabb sipped her wine and started to rub her right foot up and down his crotch. Her moisture level increased significantly when she felt his growing erection. Victor groaned and moved closer to her. He leaned over and nuzzled her neck lightly. She smelled of an exquisite fragrance that Victor was not familiar with. He treated her earlobe and neck to gentle nips with his teeth while he slowly ran his left hand up her slender thigh. Mrs. McNabb subtly opened her legs to allow him easier access. She placed the glass of wine on the small marble table next to the couch and pulled Victor to her. They kissed slowly and sensuously, tongues dancing as they explored each other's mouth. Victor grazed her mound with a solitary finger and was rewarded with a sticky wetness.

"Take me to the bedroom," she commanded huskily.

Victor easily scooped her in his arms and she directed him to the bedroom.

Victor took her into the bedroom and gently placed her on the queen size bed. The bedroom was large and decorated fully in white and marble. The entire ceiling was covered with mirrors. There was a swing of some sort with a harness to the right of the bed. It was clearly designed for sex. *Mrs. McNabb is a freak*, Victor thought as he undressed slowly while Mrs. McNabb watched him, posing sexily from her perch on the bed. When Victor was completely nude, Mrs. McNabb rose from the bed. She stood in front of the swing and instructed him to remove her dress. Victor did her bidding. She was naked underneath. Victor admired her naked form. Her small breasts were relatively firm with large erect nipples. Her stomach was flat and her curvy hips splayed sexily from her tiny waist. She sat down on the swing and adjusted it so that she was in line with his manhood.

Mrs. McNabb pulled Victor close to her and kissed his cock softly and slowly; licking him languidly with her velvety tongue. She cupped his buttocks with her hands and took his dick deeply inside her mouth. Victor moaned with pleasure and looked up at the mirrored ceiling. He watched riveted as her head bobbed up and down as his dick disappeared in her generous mouth over and over again.

Mrs. McNabb then cupped his testicles and rubbed them together in a gentle embrace. She looked up at him as she stroked his dick skillfully, applying just the right amount of pressure as she ran her nimble tongue around his scrotum; taking one, then both of his balls in her mouth. She sucked them gently, twirling them in her mouth. Victor's knees buckled.

Mrs. McNabb released his swollen member from her mouth and got up from the swing. She climbed onto the massive bed and reclined on the fluffy pillows and spread her legs wantonly, exposing every inch of her glistening sex. Her vagina was shaved with a little decorative strip at the top. Her clit was large and erect, and her labia fleshy and compact. There's a saying that slim women have fat pussies and looking at Mrs. McNabb's genitalia, Victor had to agree. He climbed onto the bed and started to lick from her ankles to her thighs, leaving a trail of wetness along her legs.

She moaned when she felt his hot breath hovering above her gaping sex. Mrs. McNabb gasped audibly when Victor inserted his rather long tongue inside her gushing orifice. Victor licked her labia almost lovingly. He tasted every inch and crevice of her pussy; sucking, nibbling and licking much to Mrs. McNabb's delight.

"Don't you dare stop," she whispered as Victor flicked his tongue against her clit in a butterfly motion. "Ohhhhh…goodness gracious…just like that."

Victor inserted two fingers and slowly moved them in and out of her hot wetness as he continued to lick her clit.

Mrs. McNabb's breathing intensified and her chest heaved as she started to ride the wave of her first orgasm of the evening. She shuddered and clenched her teeth as she squirted in Victor's mouth. Victor was surprised by the gush and got some in his eye when he raised his head in surprise.

"I forgot to warn you. I'm a squirter," Mrs. McNabb murmured, smiling.

"So I see," Victor replied dryly, wiping his eye. He had never seen anything like it.

She removed a condom from the bedside drawer and handed it to Victor. She went over to the swing and sat down while Victor put the condom on. She instructed Victor to get underneath the swing and then she lowered it, stopping mere inches from his body. The seat of the swing had a hole, rudely exposing her gaping sex. Victor adjusted himself and held his cock by the base as she lowered the swing until he was inside her. Victor groaned as she started to move the swing ever so slightly, causing delightful friction to his turgid member. They copulated like that for ten minutes and then she got back onto the bed and allowed Victor to enter her missionary style. He fucked her slowly but forcefully in a circular motion as she caressed his back and sucked his nipples, biting him occasionally. She locked her legs around his buttocks and squeezed him tightly as they moved in unison. She squeezed his cock mercilessly with her vaginal muscles. Victor groaned loudly and struggled not to climax.

"You want to come don't you," she whispered in his ear.

Victor gave an unintelligible grunt in response.

"Have you ever been inside a vagina this wet and succulent," she murmured as she raked his back with her manicured fingers.

Victor devoured her mouth as a powerful orgasm gripped his twenty-five year old body. He thrashed and writhed atop Mrs. McNabb as her pussy continued to milk him.

"Oh my god," Victor exclaimed softly, his body still shivering slightly from his thunderous explosion. "That was phenomenal."

"I hope you don't think we are through," Mrs. McNabb responded, getting up and gesturing for him to follow her. They went into her spacious bathroom and got into the Jacuzzi. They gently stroked each other's genitals for several minutes as they luxuriated in the warm, bubbly water. When Victor was sufficiently erect, she got up and placed one leg on the top of the Jacuzzi and Victor entered her from the rear. Victor inserted the head of his dick and slowly worked it in and out, teasing her extremely wet pussy which grabbed and tugged his dick as if begging it to penetrate her fully.

The water sloshed about as Victor quickened his pace, gripped Mrs. McNabb tightly by the hips and pounded her relentlessly. She arched her back and met him thrust for thrust, urging him to go deeper. Victor slapped her tiny butt as he pulled out and released his hot semen all over her lower back.

"Mmmm, I feel nice and tingly all over," Mrs. McNabb purred. "Come and join me in the shower."

Victor followed her into the shower and closed the transparent, glass door behind him. Steam filled the shower as hot water cascaded down their bodies. She lathered his body sensuously, paying special attention to his genitals. Victor did not think it was possible for him to achieve another erection. He was wrong. His cock responded like a loyal soldier to the command of her soft, knowledgeable hands. She tugged his dick artfully, varying the speed and pressure as she looked in his eyes. Victor braced against the glass door and closed his eyes. The woman was insatiable. She stroked his dick furiously until he was near orgasm. Then she abruptly stopped. She ignored his trembling erection and resumed lathering the rest of his body. When she was through they exited the shower and she dried him with a plush white towel. She instructed Victor to sit on the swing and she opened a small refrigerator that actually looked like a small table, and retrieved a bottle of whipped cream. She knelt in front of Victor and sprayed a generous amount of the cream on his genitals. Victor groaned as the icy cream made his phallus tingle with an almost painful pleasure. She then ran her tongue along the length of his now turgid member, licking off the cream and swallowing his dick with her hot mouth. Victor grunted loudly as the contrast of the cold cream and her hot mouth sent electrical surges through his body. She sucked him hungrily, greedily even. Victor held on to the sides of the swing and shouted to the mirrored ceiling as he shot a torrid load in Mrs. McNabb's benevolent mouth. She kept sucking until he was completely drained and his nerves were frayed.

"You gave a good account of yourself, young man," Mrs. McNabb said to him as they relaxed on the bed a few minutes later.

"Umm, thank you," Victor responded.

Victor checked the time. "Well, if you don't mind I'm going to take off. I need to get some rest or I'll be a mess at work tomorrow."

"Ok, no problem. I'll give you a call."

Victor dressed and left the apartment. The security guard at the gate picked up the phone and made a call as soon as Victor had driven out of the complex. Victor yawned as he headed down Jacks Hill Road, he couldn't recall the last time he had felt so tired. Mrs. McNabb had completely worn him out. When he got back to his apartment, Victor set his alarm for seven the next morning and went to bed where he promptly fell asleep.

He was awakened out of his heavy slumber by loud knocking to the door of his apartment. He groaned and looked at the time. It was 12:30 a.m. He had only been asleep for a mere half hour. Victor dragged himself out of bed and groggily made his way to the door.

"Who is it?" he asked angrily as he stood by the door.

"Hi baby," a female voice purred. "Aren't you gonna let me in?"

Victor didn't recognize the sultry voice. Who the hell was that? "Listen, whoever you are, you came at a bad time. I'm dead tired and I need to get back to sleep."

"Oh baby, you need to see what I'm wearing…just let me in and look at my sexy outfit and then if you still want me to leave I'll go," the voice replied alluringly.

Victor opened the door and a pretty girl he did not recognize stepped into the apartment. Victor was about to close the door when it was forcefully pushed in, knocking him down in the process. Victor looked up in surprise, and then fear, as two men stood over him menacingly. One was armed with a handgun and the other a baseball bat.

"So ah yuh ah fuck the big man wife," the taller of the two stated. "The big man nuh appreciate that at all."

Victor opened his mouth to say something, anything, but nothing came out.

"Big man send us to teach yuh a lesson," the short guy wielding the baseball bat advised and raised the bat to strike Victor.

"Wait!" Victor squealed in protest. "You have the wrong guy!"

"Shut up!" The man snarled. "Yuh just come from up ah de house not too long ago."

Victor peed his boxers as he realized that Mrs. McNabb's jealous estranged husband obviously had her under surveillance.

Victor screamed at the top of his lungs as the baseball bat connected with his cranium.

DANGEROUSLY IN LUST

*J*erry watched transfixed as the voluptuous young woman slid down the pole with her legs at a 180 degree angle. Her mound strained against the material of the flimsy red g-string that she was wearing. The men closest to the stage cheered and threw one hundred bills at the woman as she straightened up, signaling the end of her set. She collected the tips, her large, firm breasts bouncing invitingly as she bent down to pick up the money and strut sexily off the stage; her ample buttocks swinging from side to side as if rocking to the beat of the reggae music blaring from the club's speakers.

This was Jerry's third night at the club. In a row. A co-worker had told him about the new strip club and Jerry had decided to check it out two days ago after a particularly stressful day at the office. He had been constantly thinking of the thick, curvy, light-skinned go-go dancer since he first laid eyes on her. The woman was designed to give men headaches. She oozed sexuality through every pore. He had yet to utter a word to her though he desperately wanted to do so. He wondered if she was like some of the strippers who weren't averse to sleeping with patrons for a price. He would pay her anything.

Jerry sipped his beer and smoked a cigarette as he watched the two young women who were now gyrating on stage. He watched but his mind was on Delicious. That was her name. He had heard the DJ shout out a compliment to her over the microphone after one of her mind boggling dance moves. His heart raced as he saw her return from around the back where she had apparently gone to relax for a bit after her crowd pleasing set. He watched as she stopped to talk to a customer, smiling flirtatiously as the man placed two five hundred bills in the waist of her bikini bottom. Jerry then watched enviously as Delicious led the man by hand to the VIP lounge. It was a large, private room that one had to pay a separate cost to enter.

Jerry checked the time. Eleven-thirty. His wife must be wondering what the hell had gotten into him, coming in late from work three nights in a row. He sipped the last of his beer and left the club. He thought of Delicious as he drove home. He decided he would withdraw some money from the ATM, at least ten thousand dollars, and take Delicious to the VIP lounge. Once there he would offer her money to have sex with him. He would take the money from his personal savings so that Marjorie, his wife, would not question what the money was for.

Jerry got home at five minutes to twelve. He immediately went to the bedroom to undress.

"Jerry, what time is it?" Marjorie asked sleepily.

"A few minutes to twelve dear," Jerry responded.

"You were out drinking with the fellows again? That's three nights in a row Jerry," Marjorie said in an accusatory tone.

Jerry climbed into the bed naked and reached for his wife.

"Be quiet woman, I have something for you…" he murmured huskily.

"Jerry…what has gotten into you…" Marjorie asked, moaning as Jerry sucked on her left breast. Jerry had come home the last two nights horny as a toad and had ravaged his wife in ways he hadn't in years.

"What yuh mean," Jerry responded, nibbling on her neck. "What wrong with me wanting to sex my wife?"

Marjorie was about to respond that prior to the last two days, the last time he had given her some was Valentine's Day, and that had been four weeks ago, when Jerry claimed her mouth hungrily. Marjorie sighed and returned her husband's passionate kiss, enjoying his new found vigor but suspicious of it nonetheless.

Jerry pushed his wife's night dress up around her waist and removed her cotton panties. Marjorie spread her legs and Jerry plunged into his wife's hairy vagina with his impatient member. Marjorie gasped and clutched Jerry close as he stuck his stubby cock in and out of her at a ferocious pace. Jerry imagined it was Delicious spread eagled beneath him and groaned loudly as he felt his orgasm rapidly approaching. Jerry climaxed noisily and immediately rolled over to sleep. Marjorie got up and went into the bathroom to finish the job. She had an orgasm in three minutes. After eight years of unsatisfactory sex with Jerry, she had become quite adept at taking care of her needs. She didn't mind that Jerry was not a good lover. Her sex drive was relatively low, once a week would be good enough for her, and Jerry was a good companion and husband. He provided well for them and she was content with that. She cleaned up and went back to bed. Marjorie snuggled up against her husband and was soon in dreamland.

Jerry was distracted at work the next day. He couldn't wait to go to the club that night. Happy hour was from 7-8, Monday through Friday. He got off work at six, and after sitting in the always heavy evening traffic from Cross Roads to Half-Way-Tree road, it would be almost seven by the time he got to the club. Perfect.

Jerry worked as an administrative supervisor at a popular bakery that had four retail outlets for its products in Kingston and Spanish Town.

He called his wife as he left the office and went around to the parking lot to retrieve his car.

"Hello," Marjorie said after the fourth ring. Jerry could hear her favourite soap opera in the background.

"Hi Marj," Jerry said, "Everything ok?"

"Yeah, I'm watching Bold & the Beautiful," she told Jerry impatiently.

"Alright, later then cause I know how you are miserable when anyone interrupts you when you're watching that crap," Jerry responded.

"Yeah, later." Marjorie hung up the phone absently as she watched the drama unfold. The confrontation she had been anxiously waiting for was about to take place.

Jerry hummed along to the oldies playing on the radio as the traffic crawled along Half-Way-Tree road. He had not cheated on Marjorie in over three years. The last time had been with that little country girl with the big ass that used to work at the bakery as a secretary. The three month affair had ended when she migrated to the United States. Jerry generally had a low libido but every now and then he would meet someone who would send blood rushing to his genitals and make him feel like a sex-starved teenager. The thought of having sex with Delicious later that night had gotten him so excited that he had sported a hard-on for most the day. It had gotten so bad that he had closed his office door and masturbated. He had whispered Delicious' name as he shot his load onto the wad of sanitary napkins.

Jerry got to the club at five minutes to seven and quickly made his way upstairs.

"Yes, Jerry," the bouncer at the door greeted him as he paid the admission fee and entered the club. *Rass, I've turned into a regular*, Jerry mused as he made his way to a table near the stage. *Even the bouncer knows my name now.* A sexily clad waitress came over and took his order a few seconds after he sat down. Jerry ordered a shot of whiskey and coke, and lit a cigarette as he looked around the club for Delicious. It was now seven o'clock and the first set of dancers made their way onto the brightly lit stage. Today was called Freaky Friday and the early happy hour show was about to begin.

The trio of dancers on the stage warmed up to the latest reggae hits and displayed some acrobatic dance moves to the ever growing crowd. The men hooted and hollered as the dark-skinned girl with the humongous breasts took off her panties and laid down spread-eagled on the stage. The other two girls also removed their bikini bottoms and one of them squatted over the girl's mouth while the other proceeded to perform cunnilingus on the girl, her large ass obscenely exposed to the excited crowd. The excitement reached fever pitch when the DJ invited any male from the audience to take the stage and penetrate the girl that had her ass in the air. One brave soul who looked like he was already drunk made his way to the stage amidst loud cheers from his friends. He was handed a condom by the DJ and he dropped his trousers and placed the condom on his erection. The girl raised her head and looked around at him briefly, and then she spread her legs wider and resumed eating out the girl enthusiastically. The eager volunteer then positioned himself behind the woman and inserted his anxious cock. The girl stopped her oral assault on her co-worker's pussy and threw her legs around his waist, balancing with her hands on the floor. The crowd went wild as he plunged eagerly inside her, his face wearing an expression of pure bliss. The girl walked like a crab with the guy still embedded in her and moved over to the corner of the stage where she proceeded to balance on her head top; literally. The crowd erupted at her acrobatics. It proved to be too much for the guy and he quickened his tempo, roaring loudly as he climaxed.

Jerry shook his head at what he had just witnessed as the crowd cheered boisterously. This club was something else. He looked around. Delicious was nowhere to be seen. When the waitress came over to give him another drink, he asked her for Delicious.

"She nah work tonight enuh," the girl responded, adding when she saw the crestfallen look on his face, "But she will be here tomorrow though."

Jerry took a long swig from the bottle of beer. *Cho man*! He fumed. Jerry was so disappointed that he got up and left the club. He didn't even respond when the bouncer asked him how come he was leaving so early. Jerry got home thirty-five minutes later and told his wife a surly hi as he passed her in the living room watching T.V.

"Jerry, what's wrong honey?" she asked when she noticed his grumpiness.

"Nothing…bad day at work," he responded gruffly and went into the kitchen to get a bottle of beer.

"But you sounded just fine when I spoke to you earlier this evening," Marjorie said.

"Just drop it nuh!" Jerry snapped and went into the bedroom.

What the hell is his problem, Marjorie thought as she resumed watching the movie. Jerry was acting really strange lately. It wasn't like him to snap at her like that.

Jerry thought of Delicious as he languidly stroked his dick in the shower. His wife came into the bathroom to pee and heard Jerry groaning in the shower. She pulled the shower-curtain back and was surprised to see him masturbating.

"Jesus Christ, Marjorie!" Jerry exclaimed. "Yuh can't give me some privacy?"

Unsure of how to respond, Marjorie closed the curtain and left the bathroom. She went around to the guest bathroom to pee. She pondered her husband's erratic behaviour as she sat on the toilet. *Something is definitely up with him,* she thought.

After his wife's unwelcome intrusion, Jerry resumed his efforts and climaxed within a few minutes. He was annoyed as the explosion wasn't as satisfactory as it would have been had he not been interrupted. Jerry sat on the back patio and was feeling mellow after three more beers and a couple cigarettes. He got up and went to look for Marjorie.

She was still in the living room watching T.V.

"Sorry for snapping at you earlier baby," Jerry whispered in her ear as he hugged her from behind. "I had a stressful day at work today, that's all."

"Well, you know better than to bring your stress from work to the house Jerry," Marjorie responded.

Jerry started kissing on her neck and caressing her ample bosom.

"Jerry, yuh taking Levitra?" Marjorie asked half-jokingly.

Jerry chuckled and climbed over the sofa. He then opened Marjorie's housedress and freed her large breasts from her bra. Jerry devoured her breasts hungrily.

He then coaxed Marjorie to position on her knees on the sofa and entered her unshaved vagina with a hard thrust.

"Ohh…Delicious," he moaned, freezing momentarily when he realized that he had uttered the stripper's name aloud.

Marjorie chuckled, thinking that he was referring to the feel of her pussy.

"It sweet yuh eh Jerry," she said saucily.

Seeing that no harm was done, Jerry pursed his lips and resumed his thrusting. He panted loudly as his testicles slapped against her meaty thighs.

Marjorie held on to the back of the couch tightly as her husband pummeled her furiously. Her butt jiggled from the force of his thrusts.

Jerry closed his eyes and shuddered as he ejaculated inside his wife.

"Whew!" Jerry exclaimed as he pulled up his shorts. "I need a smoke!"

"I notice you have been smoking more than usual, you need to cut down honey," Marjorie chided her husband gently.

"Yeah baby," Jerry responded and went out to the back patio to light up.

Jerry took a deep drag as he looked out into the night. Tomorrow. He would see, and hopefully have sex with Delicious tomorrow night. He couldn't wait.

Jerry was in a buoyant mood as he and his wife went about their regular Saturday routine. He took Marjorie to the supermarket to pick up some groceries, they had lunch at a fast food restaurant and when they returned home in the early afternoon, Jerry washed the car while Marjorie unpacked the groceries and cooked red peas soup with pig tail and dumplings.

After dinner they played scrabble for an hour and then Marjorie went next door to visit their neighbour, Donna, who had recently given birth to a bouncing baby boy, leaving Jerry glued to the T.V. set. His alma mater was playing in the Manning Cup final and he was pissed at how poorly they had started the game.

"I'm going out for a bit with the fellows," Jerry casually remarked to his wife at 9 p.m. that night.

"Marky needs to get married and stop influencing you to go on the road so much," Marjorie responded. She was referring to Jerry's longtime friend who she didn't approve of because of his wild ways. Grown man still thinks he's in his early twenties she would always say whenever his name came up.

"Just easy babes," Jerry replied, "We just going to watch sports and have a few drinks." Jerry then made his way to the bathroom and took a nice long shower. He then dressed in his favourite shirt, a long sleeved blue and black stripe shirt that Marky had bought back for him from a trip to Miami late last year and blue jeans. He splashed on some Cool Water cologne and went out into the living room.

"See you later babes," he said, giving his wife a kiss on the cheek.

"Uh huh," Marjorie muttered in response. She was peeved as they usually cuddled and watched movies together on a Saturday night.

Jerry left the house and hopped in his car. *Delicious here I come*, he mused excitedly and drove out into the Saturday night traffic heading down Constant Spring Road. Jerry took out his cell phone and dialed Marky's number.

"Hello."

"Marky what's up?" Jerry asked as he waited for the traffic light to turn green.

"Nothing much, about to go Port Royal with this nice little university chick I met yesterday," Marky told him. "What yuh up to?"

"Going to the new strip club on Half-Way-Tree Road. If Marjorie call yuh don't answer yuh phone," Jerry told him.

Marky chuckled. "Yeah man, no problem."

"Alright then, link you tomorrow."

Jerry hung up and turned into the club's parking lot and eased in a spot beside a small sports car. The parking lot was almost full.

Jerry felt his excitement mounting as he paid the admission fee and entered the club. Instead of sitting at a table as usual, he stood at the bar close to the entrance to the dancer's dressing area. That way he could have easy access to Delicious whenever she was passing by.

Jerry ordered a shot of Hennessy and scanned the club. It was packed and he noticed three new dancers he hadn't seen before. He didn't see Delicious though. He looked on the action on the stage. There were two girls dancing in various states of undress. One had some sort of cow-girl costume on complete with hat and boots with her breasts hanging out while the other girl had on a nurse outfit with the already short skirt pulled up around her waist displaying her vagina in all its glory.

Jerry sipped his drink and nearly spilled it when he turned his head and saw Delicious emerge from the dancers' lounge area. She had on a black cat suit completed with a whip, mask and black thigh high fuck-me-boots. The cat suit looked as if it had been painted on. It was short and stopped just below her voluptuous ass and also showed quite a bit of cleavage. Her nipples were barely covered. She had on fire-engine red lipstick and her short hair was freshly dyed a bright blonde. She stood by the door and posed sexily as those who saw her entrance started whistling and cheering. She was the Queen of the club. Jerry almost drooled as he watched her stroll sexily pass him and head toward the stage.

"Up next is the one and only Delicious!" the DJ announced. The crowd cheered loudly as she went onto the stage.

The entire crowd watched transfixed as the DJ threw on Shaggy's new hit song and Delicious started dancing.

She cracked her whip playfully at the men closest to the stage and moved her waist in a slow sensuous motion. She licked her lips suggestively as she slowly pulled the zipper on the suit down to her crotch. The crowd went ballistic when they saw the blonde tuft of pubic hair.

"De carpet match de drapes to rass!" A man close to where Jerry was standing said much to the amusement of those who heard him.

Delicious continued her strip tease until she was now completely naked. Her nudity was a sight to behold. She was ridiculously sexy. Her measurements were 36-24-48. Those kinds of numbers will make pastors abandon their flock and make grown men lose all rational thinking. Her plump vagina was devoid of hair except for the small triangular patch just above her clit which was dyed the same colour as her hair. Jerry felt faint when she bent over during a dance move and he looked dead on into her succulent looking pink flesh. He endured a painful erection during her entire set. Jerry was on fire. He had to have her. Whatever the price.

The stage was filled with one hundred dollar bills and even some five and one thousand bills from the big spenders by the time Delicious finished her crowd pleasing set. She put back on her suit, gathered her money and exited the stage. *Here she comes*, Jerry said nervously to himself as she made her way to the dancers' dressing area, stopping briefly to speak with a couple of her many admirers.

"Ahem, Delicious," he croaked as she walked by him.

"Yes?" She looked at him questioningly. The blue contacts she was wearing made her look exotic.

"I ne…ne..need to talk to y..ou… when you come back out," Jerry stammered. He couldn't believe he was tongue-tied.

"I'll take you to the VIP lounge," he added when he saw her disinterested expression.

71

"Ok," she agreed. "I'll be out in about fifteen minutes."

"I'll wait right here."

She nodded and sauntered into the dressing room.

Jerry exhaled. He was so excited he didn't know what to do with himself. He ordered another shot of Hennessy and downed it in one go. He lit a cigarette and took a few deep drags until he calmed down. By the time Delicious returned he felt a lot more confident.

She returned looking like fresh like she had just taken a shower. She was now clad in a white bikini set and white stilettos. She went over to Jerry and stood in front of him. Close. Jerry felt the beginning of another erection. He cleared his throat.

"Ready?"

"Aren't you going to get me a drink?" she asked in a tone that suggested he should know better.

"Of course," Jerry said quickly. "What yuh drinking?"

"Get me a glass of white wine," she replied.

Jerry purchased the wine and Delicious led him to the VIP lounge. A burly bouncer looked him up and down and took the admission fee which was a whopping thousand dollars. Shit, Jerry thought inwardly, it cost half of that to get into the club!

The lighting was low in the VIP lounge and there were about ten private booths and a small bar manned by a rather young looking but very pretty dark-skinned girl. Delicious went into one of the booths on the far right and sat on the small intimate leather sofa. Jerry's heart raced as he sat beside her. Her nearness intoxicated him.

Delicious sipped her wine, running her pierced tongue suggestively along the rim of the glass. She waited for him to speak.

"Ahem...I really like you Delicious," Jerry began. "From the first time I came in the club yuh just have mi weak. You're the only reason I keep coming back."

She smiled encouragingly and Jerry continued.

"I …I…desperately want to have sex with you," Jerry said nervously. "No matter the cost." Supposed she turned him down? He didn't think he could handle that.

"Jerry, I only do that with a select few…why should I sleep with you?"

"Delicious you have an effect on me that no woman has ever had. I'll pay you well…whatever it takes!" Jerry replied with fervor.

Delicious sipped her wine and looked at him with an amused expression. She then suddenly placed her free hand on his crotch and squeezed gently. Jerry exhaled. He wasn't even aware he had been holding his breath.

"I'm very expensive Jerry," she informed him as continued to massage his genitals through his trousers.

"Anything...whatever it cost..." Jerry moaned; his eyes tightly closed.

"An hour with me will cost you seven thousand dollars and that's just for straight penetration. If you require oral sex that's an additional fifteen hundred."

"Can we do it tonight?" Jerry asked anxiously. He was struggling not to climax in his pants under her knowledgeable caress.

"Sure. You'll have to take me to a decent hotel though. I can leave the club at twelve."

Jerry breathed a sigh of relief and his heart pounded as Delicious slowly opened his zipper.

"Tip me," she instructed.

Jerry hurriedly stuffed a five hundred dollar bill in her bra.

Delicious maintained eye contact as she freed his turgid, stubby cock from the confines of his underwear.

She held his cock in her hand. It trembled.

"You want me don't you…" she whispered softly, and began to stroke him gently.

"Yes…mi want yuh bad," Jerry croaked in a strained voice.

"Can you handle this fat, sweet, juicy pussy..." she said in his ear as she massaged his scrotum while stroking his dick ever so slowly.

"Oh god…" Jerry whispered as he gripped the sofa tightly with both hands.

Delicious removed the towel that was hanging on the wall beside the sofa and held it in place as Jerry shuddered and ejaculated.

Jerry opened his eyes and looked at the towel. *Wow, that was a heavy load,* he thought.

Delicious smiled at him. "Are you sure you have another one in the chamber? Twelve o' clock is only an hour away."

"I'm positive that won't be a problem," Jerry replied confidently.

"Ok, I have another set to do so I need to get back to the dressing room," Delicious announced and stood up.

"Ok, I'll wait for you by the bar," Jerry responded.

"No, when it's twelve, leave the club and wait for me in your car," she instructed.

"Ok," Jerry agreed, though he would have liked being seen leaving the club with Delicious.

Delicious took his cell number and they headed out back to the main area of the club. She went to change and Jerry sat at a table with two lesbians and had another drink.

They completely ignored him as he listened to their banter about which girls in the club they would like to sleep with. Delicious was apparently at the top of their list. Jerry listened to one of the women intimate the things she would like to do to Delicious through Delicious' fifteen minute set. There was a slight commotion as one of the bouncers forcibly but easily removed a drunken patron who apparently had crossed the line with one of the dancers.

At the stroke of midnight, Jerry excitedly made his way out to the parking lot. He got in his car and turned the radio on as he waited impatiently for Delicious. At 12:30, Jerry was about to panic when his cell phone rang.

"I'm coming out now, where are you parked?" Delicious asked.

"Close to the entrance, I'm in a black Honda Accord," Jerry replied anxiously.

Several seconds later he watched excitedly as Delicious came into view. She had on blue hipsters jeans which hugged her hourglass figure tightly, and a pink top with pink slippers to match. Jerry tooted his horn and she came over to the car toting a small traveling bag. She looks younger without any make-up, Jerry thought to himself as he gunned the engine and drove out onto Half-Way-Tree Road.

Delicious reclined her seat, slipped off her slippers and put her feet up on the dashboard. Jerry, normally very touchy about his new car, did not comment.

"Which hotel are we going?" she asked, stifling a yawn. Her large breasts strained against the material of her blouse.

"How about Knutsford Inn?" Jerry asked, referring to one of the lower tier but fairly decent hotels in Kingston.

"Ok, I guess," Delicious responded.

They got to the hotel in ten minutes. The room had to be rented for the night, even though he would only be there for an hour. They got a room on the second floor and Jerry tried not to show how eager he was by walking to the room at a deliberately slow pace. It was now exactly three minutes to one.

They entered the room and Jerry closed the door and turned on the light. It was a typical hotel room, nothing to write home about really, but clean, the air conditioner worked and the bed looked comfortable. Jerry took out his wallet and handed Delicious $8,500.

She counted it and smiled. She knew he wouldn't have been able to resist wanting to feel her pierced, velvety tongue on his genitals. With his heart pounding loudly in his ears, Jerry unbuttoned his shirt and sat down on the bed.

Leaving the room brightly lit, Delicious deftly discarded her clothing and stood in front of Jerry with her legs slightly spread and her hands on her hips.

"Hurry up and undress, your hour began five minutes ago," she said with a smile.

Jerry broke out of his reverie and tore off his pants and boxers. Delicious approached him. She lowered her head as if to kiss him but when Jerry closed his eyes he felt her warm tongue on his neck instead. Delicious caressed his hairy chest, and sucked his nipples, giving him sharp little bites intermittently. Jerry groaned and ran his hands through her hair. Delicious left a trail of wetness as she kissed her way from his chest to his groin. Jerry balanced on the bed by his elbows and put up his legs, giving her better access to his genitals.

"Christ…" Jerry murmured when Delicious kissed the tip of his shaft and ran her lips sensuously along the sides. She gently squeezed his testicles together and slowly took the head of his phallus into her mouth.

"Oh…my…god…" Jerry moaned when he felt her tongue ring. The sensation was driving him out of his mind. Delicious slowly swallowed more of his dick until her mouth covered his cock completely.

"Lawd…Delicious…dat feel so fucking good…"

She switched gears and started sucking his dick vigorously, her head bobbing up and down as she deep throated Jerry's dick with consummate ease. She then stroked his dick expertly with her hand while she nibbled on his scrotum, resulting in Jerry emitting a variety of whimpers and grunts.

She was just about to lessen the pressure on his cock when Jerry ejaculated without warning, flooding her face with semen.

"Sorry, 'bout that," Jerry gasped, surprised that he had climaxed almost without warning. He had felt a quick sudden surge and next thing he knew semen was spewing all over Delicious' face. That blow job was just too incredible.

Delicious got up quickly and went into the bathroom. She came out with her face freshly scrubbed a few minutes later.

"You do oral Jerry?" Delicious asked him pointedly as she came to join him in the bed.

"I've never done it before," Jerry admitted. Giving cunnilingus was frowned upon by the men in his circle so he had never done it.

Delicious opened her legs widely and spread the lips of her vagina.

"Look at my juicy pussy Jerry," she purred. "Yuh sure you don't want a taste?"

Jerry gulped and fished for a condom in his trousers pocket. He had dreamt for days about sticking his dick inside Delicious and he would be damned if he would waste precious time muff diving.

Delicious watched him as he eagerly rolled on the condom. She was hoping he would've eaten her. She loved oral sex. Next time if he wanted her services, he would have to go downtown. Jerry climbed on top of her and Delicious lifted her right leg, holding it straight up in the air. Her glistening vagina gaped at him invitingly.

The visual drove Jerry crazy. He rammed his dick inside her. Delicious knew he wouldn't last long.

"You like this position Jerry," she whispered. "You like how my tight pussy choking your buddy…hmmm?"

Jerry panted loudly as he fucked Delicious like his life depended on it. He couldn't believe he was finally inside her. It was everything he thought it would be and more. He felt like he had his dick inside a small jar filled with warm, sticky honey.

"Jesus Christ…Delicious…inside ah yuh feel so good… sweet…oh god…" Jerry felt his orgasm approaching and though he desperately wanted to last longer, he just couldn't stop thrusting. Instead he increased his pace as Delicious urged him to give her all he had.

"Ohhhhhhh god…Delicioussssssssssss!" Jerry screamed as he ejaculated. As he pulled out of Delicious and removed the condom, Jerry realized that he had a serious problem on his hands. He had just picked up an expensive habit. Now that he knew how good Delicious felt he did not think he could go for long periods without being inside her. His cell phone rang, interrupting his train of thought. It must be Marjorie he thought as he walked over to the bedside table.

"Hi babes," he said.

"Jerry it's almost two o' clock! Bring your ass home!" Marjorie demanded.

"Hello Ma'am, calm down and don't talk to me like that! I'm a grown rass man," Jerry retorted, embarrassed as he was certain that Delicious had heard what Marjorie said. "I'll come home when I'm ready!"

Marjorie slammed the phone down in his ears and went back to bed. *Is alright Jerry, keep up your foolishness and see what happens*, she said to herself as she covered up and tried to go back to sleep.

Damn out of order, Jerry fumed inwardly as he sat down on the bed. He checked the time. Five minutes to two.

"Somebody is going to get a spanking this morning," Delicious teased as she got up to get dressed.

"So when can I see you again?" Jerry asked, ignoring her comment.

"Well, that depends Jerry," she replied as she pulled on her jeans. "Hold on a minute."

She dialed a number on her cell phone.

"Blacka, pick me up at Knutsford Inn in five minutes."

"I would've taken you home," Jerry told her when she got off the phone.

"No, I'm fine," she replied. "Anyways, whenever you want to see me just let me know a day in advance."

She finished getting dressed and sat on the edge of the bed. She rubbed his crotch playfully. "If you ever want me to spend a night with you, it will cost you fifteen thousand."

Immediately Jerry started to think of a plausible excuse to give Marjorie for staying out an entire night. *I'll think of something,* he mused and got up to finish putting on his clothes. Delicious' cell phone rang. She looked at the number but didn't bother to answer the call.

"My ride is here. You have my number. See you Jerry." She winked at him and left.

Ah boy, Jerry sighed. It should be a damn crime for one woman's pussy to be so sweet. His body still tingled from her touch. He buttoned his shirt, grabbed his keys and cell phone, and left the room. Jerry got home twenty minutes later and headed straight for the shower. Marjorie had woken up when his car had entered the garage but she pretended to still be asleep when Jerry had come out of the shower and got into bed. It took Jerry awhile to fall asleep as he couldn't stop thinking about Delicious.

Marjorie ignored Jerry when he strolled into the kitchen for his breakfast the following morning. She had made fried dumplings and liver, one of their usual Sunday morning fare, but she hadn't dished out any for him. He grunted a good morning to which she did not respond and helped himself. He joined her at the table and dug into his food.

"You don't think you owe me an apology Marjorie?" he asked through a mouthful.

Marjorie looked at him as if he was mentally challenged and took a deep breath to calm herself before responding.

"I won't discuss this until tomorrow Jerry," she told him coldly. "Today is a day for the Lord and a day of relaxation. By the way, be ready to accompany me to church in forty-five minutes."

Jerry groaned. All he wanted to do was to read the paper and then crawl back into bed. But he had to take her. They would be going to Donna's church today as she had invited them to a special service they were having. Marjorie got up from the table and went to get ready.

Forty minutes later, they were met outside by Donna and her baby, and they piled into Jerry's car and drove to Donna's church in Duhaney Park in relative silence, except for a few occasional sounds from the baby. It was a large Baptist church with a huge congregation. They went in and sat together in the front pew close to the choir. The choir stood up to sing a number to commence the service. Jerry looked at the lead singer and gasped in shock.

There was Delicious, minus her tongue ring, looking radiant in her gown, leading the choir in song.

She caught his eye and gave him a subtle wink.

URBAN GUMPTION

*H*igh grade! High grade!" the sweaty Rastafarian sporting a huge spliff in his mouth shouted as he slowly made his way through the thick crowd, clutching a fistful of pungent marijuana.

It was two-thirty in the morning and the session was in full swing. It was a birthday extravaganza, put on by one of Jamaica's most popular singers, Dougie Soul. A near capacity crowd was rocking to the beat of one of the three popular sound systems that were on hand for the festivities.

"Woii!" A group of scantily clad women with outrageous hairstyles shouted as they lewdly gyrated to a particularly raunchy but extremely popular song by a new artiste on the rise. The video man came over and the women tried to outdo each other in front of the video light. The women danced like seasoned go-go dancers as the video man held his lens low to catch a peek of their underwear. It wasn't difficult as three of the women had on really short skirts and made no attempt to cover up.

The tall, bow-legged, voluptuous dark-skinned girl wearing a short white skirt, standing in close proximity to the crew of women reveling in the video-light caught Terrence's roving eye. He watched as she demonstrated her dancing prowess, effortlessly moving her waistline sensuously to the infectious rhythm of the song playing.

Terrence Hill hailed from Norbrook, located in the affluent section of uptown Kingston; light years away from the innercity community from which Latesha, the woman whom he was admiring, resided. Terrence loved having sex with ghetto women. He had the requisite uptown girlfriend that men in his social circle were expected to have but he craved the primal, no-holds barred, mind boggling sex that he only experienced with ghetto girls. After listening to his best friend and fellow party animal Joshua raving over and over again about the girl he was seeing from one of Kingston's most volatile areas, he agreed to meet one of her friends. It had been an experience to remember and though he no longer saw that girl, he has since kept a ghetto girl on the side. All he had to do was provide them with a few trinkets and some spending money, and take them out occasionally in exchange for sex whenever and however he wanted it. Another thing he liked was that he could be himself around them. He could curse, drink and smoke as much as he wanted and be as freaky in bed as he desired without being judged. His girlfriend, the eldest daughter of a prominent banker, was a bit uptight and conservative.

Terrence was in full agreement with the assertion that ghetto girls 'have de wickedest slam'. The party was being held in one of the most dangerous ghettos in Kingston; however it was relatively safe for the many uptowners who attended parties there, as the gang who ran the community with an iron fist had guaranteed the safe coming and goings of all party goers.

"Look at the one in the white," Terrence said to Josh who was sipping from a small bottle of Hypnotiq.

"Yeah, she's sexy," he agreed, adding, "Nice lips…she should be able to give good head."

They both chuckled. After watching the woman for a few more minutes, Terrence casually strolled over to where she stood.

"Hi sexy," he murmured. She could hear him clearly as the disc jockey had stopped the music to make announcements of forthcoming events to be held in the community.

She appraised him before responding. With a practiced eye she quickly scoped out his designer threads, the understated but expensive jewellery adorning his hands and neck, and the large bottle of Hypnotiq in his hand.

"Hey," she finally responded.

"I've been watching you for awhile now…like the way you move that sexy body of yours," Terrence told her as he took a good look at her face. She was pretty in a rough sort of way. Nice features but too much make-up and too many late-nights partying had diminished her natural beauty. Her body looked extremely appealing though and that was what Terrence was interested in.

"Thanks," she murmured, as she waved to two women who told her hi as they walked pass.

"I'm Terrence, so what's your name?" Terrence asked, as he poured some Hypnotiq into a plastic cup.

"Latesha," she responded, "but mi friend dem call mi Buffy."

Terrence chuckled. "I wonder how you got that name…"

They both grinned.

"Guess yuh wi haffi find out," she responded cheekily.

"I'd like to see you every now and then," he told her, getting straight to the point. "I have a woman so I'm not looking anything serious but I want you to be available whenever I want to see you. Money is no object and I push an X5 so you know its all good."

"Dat can gwaan yes," she told him. "Just make sure yuh nuh beat woman cause mi nuh de pon dat."

"Don't worry yourself babygirl," Terrence told her as he whipped out his cell phone.

"Give me your number," he said.

Latesha gave him her number and he stored it.

"Buy yourself a drink," he whispered in her ear and discreetly stuffed a thousand dollar bill in her hand. "I'm going back over to my friend so I'll give you a call tomorrow."

She nodded and one of her friends came over to her as soon as Terrence left her side.

"Money boy dat enuh," she announced, adding nosily, "Him like yuh? Yuh give him yuh numba?"

"Peaches yuh too fass," Latesha responded, adding, "Yuh want anything to drink?"

"Mi woulda drink a Guiness yes," Peaches replied, somewhat peeved at Latesha for not giving her any gossip.

"Ok, come on," Latesha said and they both walked off to the bar.

"**E**verything good?" Joshua asked when Terrence returned to where he stood.

"Yeah man," Terrence replied, adding, "Guess what her nickname is?"

Joshua shook his shoulders.

"Buffy," Terrence told him.

Joshua smiled. "Pussy supposed to well fat."

"I'll soon find out how fat it is. I'm gonna call her tomorrow and take her somewhere. I'll just dodge Victoria for a few hours," Terrence told him and checked the time.

It was four in the morning.

"Remember we're going sailing to Lime Key tomorrow," he said to Josh. "Let's bounce and go get some sleep."

Joshua agreed and they both walked off to where their SUVs were parked. They usually went sailing with their girlfriends on Terrence's dad's yacht on a Sunday morning. They nodded a respectful greeting to a group of six men standing near their vehicles.

Joshua pulled off first in his black Range Rover and Terrence followed in his pearl white BMW X5 and they sped off onto Spanish Road and left the ghetto behind as they made their way uptown. They both lived in the Norbrook area but on different streets. They tooted their horns and Joshua turned onto his street while Terrence continued further up the road.

Victoria was asleep in his bed when he got home. She had her own place but she had a key to his house and slept over from time to time.

She stirred when he entered the bedroom but did not awaken. Terrence smiled to himself as he undressed. Victoria slept like a log. He looked at her sleeping form in the semi darkness. She was a pretty girl. She had an almost white, milky complexion courtesy of her mother's side of the family which was Caucasian; long, silky black hair that she wore way too often in a chignon; small perky breasts; long slender legs that went on forever and a very flat stomach. His dad wanted him to marry her and he most likely would. He didn't love her but he loved the fact that he was the only man that she had ever been intimate with and most importantly, Victoria was the type of woman that his parents expected him to start a family with. It wouldn't do to ruffle his parents' feathers where that was concerned as his dad had made it clear that he should marry her. *The old man is vindictive enough to cut me out of his will*, Terrence thought ruefully as he climbed onto the large waterbed. Barrington Hill, known in corporate Jamaica as 'The Barracuda', always got what he wanted.

Terrence snuggled up against Victoria and started getting aroused when he felt her warm body against his. Again she stirred but did not awaken. Terrence reached down and gently caressed her legs. She had gone to bed in one of his white long sleeved dress shirts. His hand wandered up to her groin and he hoped for once she wasn't wearing any underwear. No such luck. He tugged gently on the waistline of her panties and tried to pull them down her legs. His movements woke up Victoria.

"Terrence…what are you doing?" she asked, rubbing her eyes.

"What does it look like babes…I want some," he replied and resumed trying to undress her.

"Stop it…Terrence stop!" she said irritably. She was annoyed at being woken up, especially for sex.

"Why are you so damn uptight Victoria?" Terrence asked in exasperation. "Sex doesn't always have to be planned you know."

"Don't be condescending Terrence. I'm aware of that but just because you're coming from god knows where, half drunk and horny, does not mean that you can just come in and wake me up from my beauty sleep and jump my bones. You didn't even know if I was here."

Terrence sucked his teeth and turned away from her. *Victoria could be such a frigid bitch sometimes*, he fumed. Terrence got out of the bed and stormed angrily into the living room. He turned on his seventy-two inch flat screen TV. He punched 21 on the remote control and the image of a petite Latino girl performing fellatio on a muscle bound guy filled the large screen. Terrence groaned as he masturbated. Victoria got up to look for him and stopped at the doorway when she saw what he was doing. *Terrence can be so disgusting at times* she thought and went back to bed. She curled up under the covers and thought about Terrence. She knew that he thought that she was frigid and had a low libido but the truth was that he didn't rock her world so she rarely had sex with him. He also thought that he was the only man she had ever been with. Silly rabbit.

Victoria wasn't in bed when Terrence woke up the next morning. He looked at the time. It was 9:30. He picked up the cordless phone and dialed her cell number.

"Hello," Victoria answered breathlessly.

"Yeah, where are you?" Terrence asked.

"I'm out jogging," she replied.

"So you don't want to go sailing this morning?"

"No, I'm not in the mood."

You're never in the mood for anything, Terrence thought irritably. "Ok, later."

Terrence hung and called Joshua.

"What's up T?" Joshua said, yawning.

"Victoria really getting on my nerves man," Terrence complained. "First she didn't want to have sex with me last night and now she's gone jogging saying she's not in the mood for any sailing."

Joshua chuckled. "Don't let Vickie stress you out, T. You know how she is sometimes. Just call the filly you met last night and go chill with her for a few hours. Later we catch up and go watch the big match at the National Stadium."

Jamaica had a friendly international football game with Argentina that evening at 4 p.m.

Joshua heard his doorbell and went to answer the door. He was only wearing his boxers and socks but he knew who it was.

"Yeah, for real. Alright I'll do that. So what are you up to?"

Joshua opened the door and Victoria, wearing black tights, designer trainers and a white T-shirt, stepped in and closed the door behind her. She gave Joshua a devilish smile and squatted in front of him.

"Hmmm, going to read the paper and then chill out at the pool for a bit. Probably call over a chick," Joshua replied, as Victoria removed his rapidly growing erection from his boxers.

"Alright, cool. Link you later," Terrence said and hung up the phone.

"Mmmmmm," Joshua moaned appreciatively as Victoria kissed the head of his dick and licked around the tip sensuously. Joshua removed the hair pin that was holding her lengthy hair in one, allowing it to flow down past her shoulders. He then grabbed a fistful of her hair and gently slid his dick in and out of her benevolent mouth. She cupped his testicles and sucked him harder.

"Yes…Vickie…just… like… that…"

The loud slurping sounds that she emitted as she greedily gobbled his phallus drove Joshua crazy. She was really into it. *If Terrence only knew what an animal his girl was in bed*, Joshua mused, not in the least bothered about having an affair with his best friend's woman. If one looked in the dictionary for the definition of dog, they would see Joshua's picture next to the word sporting a proud smile.

"Don't stop...yeah baby..." Josh groaned as Victoria stroked his dick with her soft hands while she licked and sucked his rather large testicles.

Victoria then stood up and pulled her tights and panties to her ankles, freeing one leg for leverage. She then bent over the arm of the couch and Josh quickly got behind her. He inserted his throbbing cock inside her pulsating wetness slowly. Victoria groaned and arched her back.

"Your cock feels so good Josh," she purred. "Fills me up just right."

Joshua's deceased father looked at them with a slight grin from the large oil painting on the wall behind them as Josh drove his dick slowly but firmly inside her.

Victoria slung her right leg on the arm of the couch and Josh responded by increasing his tempo. They had been having a passionate affair for eleven months now. It had started one week after she had met Terrence at a cocktail party the French Ambassador to Jamaica had put on at the consulate.

"Harder! Faster! Give it to me Josh!" Victoria implored, backing up against him and meeting his furious thrusts.

"Oh Vickie…oh Vickie…oh Vickie…" Joshua moaned as he pounded her tight, wet pussy, sweat dripping off his body onto her back.

"I want to ride you," Victoria told him breathlessly.

Still embedded in her, Joshua held her and they crumbled to the plush tan carpet. She rode his dick with her back to him. Joshua panted as he watched his shiny dick disappear inside her over and over again. Victoria squeezed her firm breasts and shook her head from side to side as she bounced up and down his shaft like it was a trampoline. Victoria then leaned her torso forward, placed her hands on the floor and continued bouncing her ass up and down on his dick. Joshua howled with pleasure.

Victoria's movements became a blur as she rapidly rode his cock to the tune of her intense orgasm. Joshua closed his eyes and savoured the feeling of her juices bathing his throbbing dick over and over again.

"Sweet…gentle…Jesus…" Victoria whispered as she shuddered repeatedly. When her spasms finally subsided, they positioned on their sides with Josh inside her from behind.

"You're so wet," Joshua murmured in her ear as he gave her slow, deep strokes.

"All for you baby," she whispered back, "all this sweetness is yours…anytime…you…want…it."

Joshua grunted and held her tightly as he started bucking like a wild horse, signaling his approaching climax.

"Let it go baby," Victoria urged. "Flood me with that big load of spunk!"

"Ohhh… God…Vickie…Jesus Christ!" Josh blasphemed as he spilled his hot semen into Victoria's willing orifice.

"That was pretty hot," Victoria remarked, as she turned to face him. Joshua's eyes were closed. He was still recovering.

"Mmmmm," he murmured in agreement. Victoria smiled and kissed him. Their sessions were always passionate. She just had to look at Joshua and she'd get horny. She then got up and went into the bathroom to take a quick shower. She put the heat control on lukewarm and lathered herself. She thought about her illicit relationship with Joshua as she cleansed her body. When Terrence had introduced her to his best friend, the chemistry between them had been palpable and instantaneous. She had literally felt her pussy jump when they had shaken hands. She had made the first move and called him two days later. He had concurred that the strong attraction was definitely mutual and that he was willing to act on it whenever she was ready. She was ready that very night and they had a very intense quickie in the back of his Range Rover outside Terrence's house. Terrence had not been feeling well and was asleep. Victoria sighed and dried herself. Life was so unfair. Why couldn't Terrence make her feel like Joshua did?

Terrence went for breakfast at Marge's, which had a very popular Sunday morning brunch. He put together a meal of steamed calaloo, fried dumplings, assorted fresh fruits and strong black coffee from the all you can eat buffet. He spotted some acquaintances at a table and joined them. The four men and lone woman conversed about sports, lamenting on Jamaica's failure to make it the World Cup Finals. An hour later, Terrence left the restaurant and called Latesha.

"Hello," she said after the fifth ring.

"Latesha, its Terrence," he said, "I want to see you today."

"What time?" she asked.

"About twelve, meet me at York Plaza in Half-Way-Tree," Terrence told her.

"Alright, later then." Latesha ended the call and resumed braiding her little sister's hair.

After leaving Joshua's house, Victoria had let Joshua give her a ride to her apartment instead of going back over to Terrence's. She was now at home waiting for her nail technician to show up for an eleven-fifteen appointment.

"Sorry I'm late, Ms. Levy," Maureen, the nail technician, apologized when she arrived at eleven-thirty.

"Spare me, you people are so irresponsible. No respect for other people's time," Victoria bristled as she led the way to the patio.

If it wasn't one thing I'd just tell this stuck-up woman bout her rass and go back home enuh, Maureen fumed inwardly as she followed Victoria. *Just because she have money she gwaan like she better than me.*

Maureen sighed as she stood outside Victoria's apartment and waited for her boyfriend to pick her up. The manicure and pedicure had taken three and a half hours during which she had endured an endless stream of criticism from Victoria. The woman could not be pleased. The bitch hadn't even given her a tip.

Terrence bopped his head to 50 Cent's new album as he waited in the parking lot for Latesha to show up. It was now ten minutes past twelve and he was getting impatient. He thought she would've been here waiting for him. When he had called her a few minutes ago, she had told him she just left her house and was on her way.

Five minutes later, Terrence glanced to his right and saw Latesha strutting sexily towards his vehicle. She was wearing a very tight, short denim shorts showing off her sexy bow-legs and hour-glass figure; baby blue sandals and a matching baby blue T that read *Heartbreaker*. Terrence looked at her crotch and saw physical evidence of why Latesha was called Buffy. He felt a stirring in his loins.

Latesha walked up to the passenger side and got in the luxurious vehicle.

"Hi," she said to Terrence.

"Hi Buffy," Terrence responded.

They both grinned.

"So, whey we ah go?" Latesha asked.

"We are going to get some food and then go to a hotel," Terrence replied as he drove out of the plaza. "What would you like to eat?"

"Lobster and shrimp," Latesha replied without hesitation.

Terrence chuckled inwardly. Get it while you can girl, get it while you can.

Terrence rubbed her leg as he whipped the SUV down the clear stretch of road leading to Port Royal.

"You're looking real sexy, Latesha," he told her over the music. "Can't wait to sample the goods."

"Mek sure you can handle de ride," she replied saucily, reaching over to give his crotch a slight squeeze. She was surprised to feel that he was erect.

"I've had an erection from the minute I saw you walking towards the van," Terrence said, grinning.

"Yuh really horny man!" Latesha exclaimed. "When last yuh have sex?"

Terrence merely laughed.

They arrived at their destination and Terrence led her to a table out on the deck so they could eat at the seaside.

"Out here really nice," Latesha commented, as they waited for their order to arrive.

"First time?" Terrence asked, surprised. Port Royal was a popular seafood spot.

"Yeah, mi neva come out yah yet," she replied.

There were six other couples in the restaurant. Terrence recognized one of the women. Joshua used to date her a few months ago. Terrence chuckled to himself. He was sure Joshua had slept with half the women in Kingston.

Their food arrived twenty minutes later and Latesha dug into her expensive meal with gusto. Terrence had a steamed parrot fish with bammy while Latesha had lobster and shrimp served with white rice. All he could think about was ravaging Latesha's voluptuous frame. He couldn't tell the last time he was so anxious to fuck someone.

He finished eating before Latesha and had a light beer while he waited for her to polish off her meal which she seemed to be enjoying thoroughly. Fifteen minutes later, Terrence paid the bill with his credit card and they left the restaurant.

Terrence drove quickly back into town and headed to Caribbean Dreams, one of Kingston's finest hotels and one of his favourite places to take women. He even had a favourite room.

"Hello, Mr. Hill," the receptionist greeted him pleasantly, totally ignoring his companion.

"Hi, is 207 available?" he asked, reaching in his wallet for his credit card.

"Let me see…yes it is," she replied.

"Good, one night," Terrence told her.

The receptionist processed his card and handed Terrence his room key.

"Enjoy," she said, a smirk playing at the corners of her mouth.

Terrence smiled and led Latesha to the elevator. He hadn't seen Anita in awhile; apparently she had been transferred back to the front desk. He had met her at a pool party two months ago and they had gone out a couple times.

They entered the large, air-conditioned room and Latesha excused herself and went into the bathroom. Terrence immediately undressed and got on the bed. He stroked his semi-erect cock as he waited for Latesha to return.

He gasped audibly when she emerged from the bathroom.

She stood naked in front of him and allowed him to feast his eyes on her exquisite body. Terrence's eyes roved from her firm, mouthwatering breasts down to her flat stomach which was adorned with a gold navel ring, then on to the abundance of clean-shaven flesh gaping prominently between her bow-legs. Terrence groaned and hoarsely commanded her to join him on the bed.

Laetsha smiled and climbed on top of him. Terrence growled and rolled them over until he was on top. He kissed her hungrily as he caressed her breasts. Latesha wrapped her legs around his lower back and nibbled on his earlobe.

Terrence kissed her hard on the neck and shoulder, leaving a trail of red marks. He sucked her breasts like a new born baby as Latesha writhed beneath him, raking his back with her long nails.

Terrence grunted in pleasure. She liked it rough; a woman after his own heart. He kissed her stomach and tugged on her navel ring with his teeth as he worked his way down to her groin. He moaned loudly as he admired her pussy. It was the plumpest he had ever seen. The girl had an embarrassment of riches between her legs. He couldn't resist. He buried his face inside her wetness.

"Mmmmm...mmmmm...mmmmmm" Latesha moaned, rubbing his head like a crystal ball as he explored her pussy with his tongue.

"So...fleshy...so...sweet..." Terrence muttered as he feasted on Latesha's vulva.

Latesha threw her legs on his shoulder and humped his mouth as she got ready to climax.

"Woii…mi ah go cum…lawd gad…" she croaked as Terrence licked her engorged clit furiously.

Latesha squealed with pleasure as she climaxed, flooding his mouth and face with her juices.

Terrence kept going, forcing another orgasm to grip Latesha just as the first was subsiding.

"Rass…one more…oh gad…" she whimpered in disbelief.

Terrence finally raised his head and rolled over. Latesha slid down and attacked his throbbing cock. She devoured it greedily. Moaning and slurping as she sucked him like his cock was the sweetest thing she had ever tasted. Terrence squirmed on the bed as Latesha worked her magic. She grabbed his legs and held them up in the air as she licked him from his anus to his scrotum, emitting loud appreciative grunts from Terrence.

"That feel so fucking good…damn…girl you're too bad…ooohhh"

Latesha then slid over to the side of the bed and got a condom from Terrence's pants pocket. She ripped off the wrapper and placed the condom in her mouth. Terrence watched excitedly as she used her mouth to skillfully roll the condom onto his dick. *Damn, this one is a keeper*, Terrence thought as he watched her climb on top of him.

Latesha inserted his dick and started to gyrate slowly as if moving to a slow, sensuous beat playing in her head. Terrence slapped her ample ass she milked his cock with her knowledge-able pussy.

"Lord…have…mercy…how yuh can fuck so…" Terrence asked rhetorically as he closed his eyes and enjoyed the sensations flowing through his body.

Latesha then slowly stepped up the pace until she was riding his cock at lightning speed.

"Tek fuck bwoy," Latesha declared nastily as she bounced up and down his turgid shaft. "No gal caa wuk yuh like me."

Terrence grunted loudly and rolled them over. He then placed her legs on his shoulders and fucked her hard and fast.

"Harder!" Latesha commanded, slapping him hard on his buttocks. "Fuck it lakka fi yuh!"

Terrence eyes rolled to the back of his head as he felt his orgasm building up. Some men would probably be turned off by Latesha's ghetto vernacular but it turned him on immensely. He threw her legs way back past her ears and plunged inside her at a ferocious speed.

"Dig mi out!" Latesha begged loudly as Terrence grunted through clenched teeth.

Terrence emitted a guttural roar as he shot a torrid load into the latex condom. He shuddered as his climax seemed to go on long after his ejaculation.

Terrence removed the condom and staggered to the bathroom to dispose of it. He then rejoined Latesha on the bed.

"Yuh alright babes?" Latesha asked, stroking his chest lightly.

"Yeah," Terrence replied, still trying to catch his breath. "I'm fucking great."

Latesha laughed.

"Listen to me girl," Terrence said, propping up by his elbows. "If you have a man, you're going to have to leave him. I don't want anybody else fucking you. Anything you want, I will provide."

Latesha looked at him but didn't respond.

Terrence continued. "I'll put you up in a nice little apartment uptown and make sure that all your needs are met."

"How does that sound?" He prompted when she remained silent.

"Mi wi think 'bout it," Latesha said finally.

Terrence was surprised she didn't jump at the offer.

"What's there to think about? What…you're not feeling me?"

"Yeah, mi like yuh…yuh look good and have money an' t'ing but inna one situation like dat yuh might try fi control mi and mi is a girl whe…"

"All I'll expect is that you only have sex with me and that you're available when I need you, that's all," Terrence told her, cutting her off in mid-sentence.

"Alright," Latesha responded, nodding. "Mek we see how it go then."

"Good, so that's settled. My family owns an apartment complex on Lady Musgrave road and one of the tenants in one of the studios is leaving at the end of this month. So in another two weeks you'll be able to move in," Terrence said and inserted his finger inside her, signaling that he was ready for round two.

Terrence's cell phone rang at three-thirty. It was Joshua.

"What's up J?" Terrence asked, through a mouthful of bar-beque chicken. He had ordered some food as they had worked up quite an appetite.

"Where are you?" Josh asked. "Remember we are taking the girls to the football match."

"Shit! I didn't remember a thing about the game," Terrence said. "I'm over by the hotel with Buffy."

Joshua laughed. "That fat pussy have you weak already."

"Whatever man," Terrence told him, laughing.

"So what then, you're not coming?" Joshua asked, no way he was going to miss the game. Its not every day one gets to watch Argentina live in action.

"I think I'm gonna miss it, I'm well relaxed in bed right now," Terrence told him as he looked over at Latesha who was sitting cross-legged, naked, munching on a drumstick.

"Ok, by the way, Vickie called me asking for you. She said she has been trying to reach you last couple of hours," Joshua told him.

"Yeah, I saw the missed calls. I'll buzz her later."

They made plans to meet up at Murphy's, a popular sports bar, for drinks after the game and hung up.

Terrence and Latesha left the hotel at six-thirty p.m. and Terrence paid for a cab to take her home. He also withdrew money using the hotel ATM and gave her ten thousand dollars pocket money; 'loose change' as he called it.

Terrence arrived at the sports bar before Joshua. He sat at the bar and sipped on a beer, watching basketball while he waited. Joshua arrived ten minutes later and much to his surprise, with Victoria in tow. *We hadn't said anything about the girls joining us, and if Vickie is here, then where is Angela, Josh's girlfriend?* Terrence thought, perturbed.

"Hi baby," Terrence said with a forced smile when they came over.

"Hey yourself," she replied coolly. "I've been calling you all day. Haven't you seen all the missed calls?"

"Baby, just relax," Terrence said soothingly, "I had left my phone in the truck while I was handling some business."

"So Jamaica managed to draw the game," he said to Joshua, trying to change the subject.

"Yeah, it was a good game. Lots of exciting moments," Joshua responded.

"So what are you doing here anyway Vickie?" Terrence asked, looking at her curiously.

"I noticed how you just changed the subject after giving me that flimsy excuse but its ok," Vickie told him with a smug expression. "It doesn't matter anymore."

"What do you mean? Stop tripping Victoria…what are you saying?" Terrence asked, getting annoyed.

"I'm leaving you for Josh, Terrence," Victoria announced matter-of-factly. "I'm tired of running around behind your back. It's over."

Terrence was stunned. He sat on the stool and looked at them with a stupid expression as his brain struggled to come to terms with what Victoria had just told him.

Terrence looked at Joshua and Joshua shrugged his shoulders nonchalantly as if to say, hey man, tough luck.

Terrence jumped off the stool and grabbed Joshua by the neck. Patrons scattered and the security came running as the two men wrestled each other to the floor.

"Terrence! Stop acting like a child!" Victoria shouted; her cheeks red with embarrassment.

The two security guards reached the men as they both scrambled to their feet and pulled their licensed firearms. The security guards jumped back and told the guys to cool it before the situation got any worse.

Terrence's eyes were red with rage and his hand shook as he held his gun level with Joshua's chest.

Joshua was calm but breathing heavily from the brief tussle. He held his gun but it was pointed to the floor. He decided to try and talk some sense into Terrence.

"Just walk away Terrence," Joshua said to him. "It's not worth it man. Put the gun away and we'll talk...we go way back, man. You pull that trigger and then what?"

"Fuck you Josh! Don't call my fucking name! You and the little bitch take me for a fool but it nah go so!" Terrence shouted.

Sirens were heard approaching the sports bar when Terrence's gun went off. Joshua crumbled to the floor and Victoria ran over to him screaming. One of the security guards tackled Terrence, trying to disarm him. Terrence fell but managed to squeeze off two more shots; one of which struck Victoria in the side.

The police burst inside and took control of the situation. They took Terrence away in cuffs and rushed Joshua and Victoria to the hospital.

A young reporter who freelanced for one of Jamaica's two television stations, scribbled on a notepad furiously as he hurried to his car. A love triangle gone bad involving the son of the powerful and wealthy Barrington 'The Barracuda' Hill was breaking news and he had the inside scoop! This was the break he had been waiting for.

ORDINARY PEOPLE

*R*haatid! Chicken price raise again?!" Ms. Tiny, as she was known to everyone in the small, countryside village called White Horses, demanded angrily. "Every minute something raise! How poor people must survive?"

"Go complain to de government Ms. Tiny," Maas Joe, the shopkeeper snapped. He was tired of people acting like he could anything about the damn economy. "Yuh either tek it or leave it."

Ms. Tiny grumbled and searched through her pockets to see if she had any more money. She found eighty dollars.

"Gimme two pounds ah de chicken back, man, and doah feisty wid me," Ms. Tiny shouted. Her loud, coarse voice belied her delicate four-foot-two-inch frame.

Maas Joe sucked his teeth and bit back a retort. Arguing with Ms. Tiny was futile. No one won an argument with the garrulous, foul-mouthed woman. He wrapped the chicken and gave it to her. Ms. Tiny gave him the evil eye as she paid him and left.

Ms. Tiny sweated profusely as she walked the mile back to her small, one bedroom board-house. The midday sun was at its peak. Ms. Tiny mopped her brow with a large rag and muttered a terse hello to Slim Jim, who was passing by on his donkey. It was rumored that his penis was larger than his donkey's. Ms. Tiny did not like him as she had made a pass at him at the fish fry held on the riverside two months ago and Slim Jim had flatly rejected her brazen advance, telling her that 'she too likkle and mawga, him like him woman dem plump and juicy'. Ms. Tiny had been embarrassed and had told him some choice words much to the amusement of the crowd.

Ms. Tiny got home a few minutes later, hot and bothered, and placed the chicken on the kitchen counter. The kitchen was a small board structure a few meters from the rear of the house. She then got some water to drink and plopped down gratefully on the wooden chair under the large, Julie mango tree. She kicked off her worn sandals as she luxuriated in the shade.

She wondered if she should take a quick bath at the river. The section of the river that was close to her house was usually cool as that area was heavily shaded by the large trees on both sides of the river. She decided she would take a nice bath to cool down and then relax for a couple hours before starting dinner. She planned on cooking curry chicken-back with dumplings and dasheen. After dinner she would send the little boy next door to go and call Quashie, for him to come to satisfy her other hunger.

Ms. Tiny went inside the house and retrieved a bar of soap, a wash cloth and a large T-shirt that had seen better days, and made the short trek down to the river.

Stanley was relaxing at the root of a tree on the hillside, rolling a spliff, when he heard a sound down by the river. He watched excitedly as he saw Ms. Tiny place her things on a large rock and start to undress. She was small and bony, her breasts barely a handful with large nipples. The thick mass of pubic hair and her weather-beaten face were the only things betraying the fact that she was not a child.

Stanley became instantly erect. He had always heard Quashie, Ms. Tiny's on-again-off-again lover, brag about Ms. Tiny's prowess in the bedroom. 'She likkle but she tallawah!' he would croak loudly after several shots of white rum. He wondered if Ms. Tiny would give him some. He watched as she lathered her petite body, humming the tune of the popular song that had won the nationwide song contest a few weeks ago. When she placed the rag between her legs and slowly rubbed it up and down, Stanley spilled the marijuana in the bush. *Cho rass!* he exclaimed in a loud whisper. He dusted off his hands and watched Ms. Tiny for a few more seconds. He then slowly made his way down to the river.

"**H**ello, Maas Joe," Precious said to the shopkeeper as she entered his shop. Precious Smith had recently moved to the community to live with her grandmother. The voluptuous twenty year old was driving the men in the community crazy. They all vied for her attention. She was originally from Old Harbour, in St. Catherine, but had re-located to White Horses to lay low because the vengeful family of a woman's husband that she had an affair with was looking for her.

"Howdy Precious," Maas Joe said with a big grin. It was rumored that Precious was sleeping with Mr. Brown who taught English, at St. Thomas Junior High, but that Slim Jim had also entered the equation. Apparently Precious had passed him peeing at the side of the road and when she saw his manhood she had taken him into the mango grove and according to what she told Pansy, the village gossip, had gotten the ride of her life.

"Maas Joe, I need a chicken and some other items," Precious said, resting her elbows on the counter as she leaned over, showing a generous amount of cleavage.

Maas Joe swallowed as he imagined sucking and caressing her mouthwatering breasts. His fifty year old cock twitched in his old cotton briefs.

"I want them on credit though," Precious said, giving his hand the slightest of touches. "Is that ok?"

"Yeah man," Maas Joe replied earnestly, "Dat is quite alright."

Maas Joe was generally regarded around White Horses as the meanest man in the village. He never gave any credit regardless of the circumstances. It was also said that he had a lot of money stashed away in a large trunk in the back of his shop. Precious was very interested to find out if there was any truth to those rumors. With the right amount of cash she could leave White Horses and relocate back to civilization. Very few people had electricity and inside plumbing, the road was in a deplorable state, no real social scene…this place was not for her. If it wasn't for big wood Slim Jim to rock her world, she would've probably gone crazy already. She just needed some good money and White Horses could kiss her big ass. Maas Joe was the key. Mr. Brown didn't make enough on his teacher's salary to take care of her, and broke ass Slim Jim was only good for one thing.

"So, Maas Joe," Precious began, smiling seductively. "How come yuh never invite me round the back to have a drink with you?"

Maas Joe's eyes widened at her words. "Mi never t'ink say a sexy girl like you woulda interested inna one old man like mi."

"I want to settle down with a nice older man," Precious told him. "Mi tired of the young bruk pocket man dem. They can't take care of a nice girl like me."

Maas Joe's knees felt weak. He couldn't believe he had a shot at bedding Precious. He smiled a toothless grin.

"Anytime yuh want to come Precious," he told her excitedly, "My door is always open to yuh."

Ms. Tiny had been rubbing her vagina furiously with the soapy rag, her eyes tightly clenched, when she felt someone's presence.

She opened her eyes.

"Stanley, whey yuh a watch mi fah?" she asked, making no attempt to cover up. Her clit was throbbing and she was annoyed at being disturbed. Another minute and she would have climaxed.

"Yuh look like yuh in heat Ms. Tiny," Stanley said pointedly. "Mi woulda love fi cool yuh dung."

Ms. Tiny chuckled. "But a wha do dis likkle bwoy doah lawd. Yuh tink say mi ah likkle pickney Stanley? Yuh caa manage dis."

Stanley dropped his tattered trousers in response.

Ms. Tiny was impressed. He wasn't as big as Slim Jim but if Slim Jim could be compared to a donkey, Stanley could be compared to a mule. She wondered how so many big wood men could be in one little village. Her sometime lover, Quashie, was no slouch in that department either.

Ms. Tiny's eyes remained rooted at Stanley's groin, her mouth slightly open.

Stanley took her silence as consent and stepped out of his pants. He was already shirtless.

He stepped in the water and moved towards her.

Ms. Tiny dipped the wash cloth in the river and rinsed the soap off her body.

She turned to Stanley and jumped in his arms. They were standing knee deep in the water. He held her easily.

She slid downwards until she felt his large member nudging the slippery entrance to her hairy orifice.

He entered her and she continued downwards until he was balls deep.

Ms. Tiny moaned with pleasure. She felt deliciously filled.

She gripped him tightly and started bouncing up and down his turgid shaft.

"Woii...lawd...yuh cocky big nuh rass..." Ms. Tiny muttered appreciatively. Ever since she had lost her virginity twenty years ago, ironically the year Stanley was born, she had a preference for well-endowed men.

Stanley lifted her up in the air and his cock slipped out of her wetness with a loud plop. He then made her stand and bend over holding on to a rock. He got behind her and slid his dick inside her with a firm thrust.

Ms. Tiny grunted loudly as Stanley turned up the pressure.

"Yuh still say mi caa manage yuh...eeh?" he asked smugly as he pounded her petite body.

"Mine yuh bruk mi inna two Stanley," Ms. Tiny warned through her pig-like grunts.

She held on to the rock for dear life as Stanley fucked her just the way she wanted to be fucked. Hard and fast.

"Yes Stanley!..uggghhh… same way so!" Ms. Tiny bellowed; her eyes tightly closed.

"Woiiii…Stanley…woiii…!" she wailed as she climaxed. She had her orgasm not a moment too soon as Stanley, still thrusting powerfully, ejaculated inside her mere seconds later.

Quashie was right, Stanley thought as he leaned against the rock to catch his breath. Ms. Tiny can really take a good pounding.

Ms. Tiny sighed contentedly and took up her wash cloth to take another bath.

"Dat hit de spot Stanley," she told him as she soaped her body. "Every now an' den yuh can come check mi."

"Alright, cool den," Stanley responded and walked to the river bank to retrieve his trousers.

"So what time yuh closing up the shop tonight?" Precious asked Maas Joe as she collected the bag with the groceries.

"Bout seven," Maas Joe replied. He usually closed at nine but if closing early meant that he would see her sooner than later, then so be it.

"Ok, I might come check yuh 'bout eight o' clock or so," Precious told him with a smile. She then left with the groceries. *Bwoy, when man think wid de wrong head it always get dem inna problem*, she mused as she met up with Slim Jim, who gave her a ride home on his donkey.

"Mi ah come check yuh back fi some dinner lata," Slim Jim told her as they made their way to the small, two bedroom structure that Precious' grandmother had owned for almost thirty years.

"Ok, I'll leave some for you," Precious agreed, adding, "I have to go take care of something lata though so mi caa hang out with you tonight."

"Where yuh going?" Slim Jim asked irritably. He was looking forward to some nice sex after dinner.

"Slim, yuh love mi?" Precious asked him suddenly.

Slim stopped the donkey.

"Of course mi luv yuh gal!" he proclaimed emphatically.

"Will you do anything for me?"

"Anyt'ing!" Slim Jim responded without hesitation.

"I have a plan, Slim. I'm going to get friendly with Maas Joe and find out if him really have a trunk full ah money. If is true, we rob him and run way and go start a new life together," Precious told him quietly. They say 'bush 'ave ears' and in White Horses, that was most certainly true. There were hardly any secrets in the small village.

She continued. "How that sound? Yuh want fi run away wid mi?"

Slim Jim choked up. "Yuh know say ah long time mi want a nice ooman fi married to...and look 'ow God just send yuh to mi! Just tell mi what yuh want mi fi do Precious."

"Good," Precious responded. *Boy that was easy*, she mused as Slim Jim grinning from ear to ear slapped the donkey and they resumed their journey to her grandma's home.

Later that night, Maas Joe closed his shop promptly at seven and refused to serve Benjie, who was just coming in from Morant Bay and wanted a tin of corn beef to cook with some dumplings for a late dinner.

"Since when yuh lock up so bloodclaat early?" Benjie demanded angrily. He was hungry and was in no mood for any foolishness.

"I lock my fucking shop any rass time ah feel like it!" Maas Joe responded from inside.

"Maas Joe, just sell me the tin ah corn beef and mek mi gwaan ah mi yaad nuh man!" Benjie said, exasperated.

"Mi say de shop lock! Come back tomorrow," Maas Joe said, as he closed the window.

Benjie trembled in anger when Maas Joe closed the window without serving him.

Whey mi ah go cook now, Benjie groaned inwardly. He was famished. He turned away from the shop and slowly made his way home. He took a shortcut and paused when he saw two silhouettes passing on the road close to the thicket he was making his way through.

He watched as they passed by. It was Precious and Slim Jim on Slim Jim's donkey. He had heard that Slim Jim was fucking her. Lucky bastard, Benjie thought as he continued home. He would have to eat boiled dumplings and butter that night.

Maas Joe took a long bath and put on his cologne that he only used on special occasions. He was also wearing new white cotton briefs and a new shirt that his son, Alwin, had sent for him from England last Christmas. He waited impatiently for Precious to arrive.

"**M**ek sure yuh nuh have sex wid him enuh," Slim Jim mumbled to Precious when he stopped the donkey so that she could get off. They were about fifty meters from the shop.

"Lawd, Slim," Precious responded derisively. "Just relax yuhself. Yuh really t'ink say mi woulda wuk that deh old man?"

"Just mek sure," Slim warned. "Cause mi wi chop up him bloodclaat if him touch yuh. Ahoa."

"I'll meet yuh right here in about an hour or so. If yuh don't see me just wait till ah come," Precious instructed him as she smoothed down the short dress she was wearing. Just looking at her gave Slim Jim a turgid erection.

"Alright, hurry up an' come back," he said, treating her to a lustful gaze.

Precious then sauntered off to the back of the shop and knocked on Maas Joe's side door, which was one of three entrances to his house.

Maas Joe got up excitedly and opened the door.

He smacked his lips as he gazed at Precious' voluptuous body spilling out of the short, tight dress.

"Good night, Precious. Come in," he said graciously, opening the door and gesturing for her to enter. The room was a bit musky, as Maas Joe kept his windows and doors closed most of the time. An ugly red and black sofa was in front of a twenty-five inch TV, one of two in the small village, Mr. Brown, the school teacher, owned the other. There was a framed photograph on the wall of a smiling big-eared young man, his son Alwin, and there was a large glass case by the wall which was home to Maas Joe's best cutlery and dishes.

He gestured for Precious to have a seat on the sofa.

"So what yuh want to drink?" he asked excitedly, as his gaze lingered on the generous amount of thigh on display.

"White rum and Pepsi," Precious responded.

He hurried to make her the drink. He handed it to her and sat next to her, sipping from the concoction he had blended together in anticipation of getting lucky tonight. It was a blend of Irish moss, linseed, guiness and eggs. It was supposed to give him stamina. He hoped it worked. This young filly was as fit they came.

Precious took several sips of the drink. He had made it strong but poor Maas Joe wouldn't know that she could knock them back with the best of them. Her father had been an alcoholic and she had been exposed to alcohol quite early.

She placed a hand on his thigh.

He smiled excitedly, exposing his gums and took a big sip from his frothy glass, leaving traces of its contents on his upper lip.

"So, Maas Joe," Precious began, "Yuh want to be the man that love mi and take care of mi?"

"Yes, Precious," he responded hoarsely as her hand crept slowly up his thigh.

"I'm a good-looking woman Maas Joe and pretty women deserve nice things, nuh true?" she asked as she lightly caressed his groin.

Maas Joe could only manage a nod. His cock was harder than it had been in twenty years. He hoped she freed it from the confines of his briefs soon; it felt like it was going to burst.

"Yuh sure yuh have enough money fi take care ah mi Maas Joe?" she asked as she pulled his zipper down slowly.

"Yes…mi…'ave …nuff…money…" Maas Joe breathed.

"Show mi de money, Maas Joe," Precious said as she held his phallus in her fist. "Show me and then we can get down to business."

Maas Joe hopped up with his dick jutting from his fly and led the way to the bedroom. He hurriedly took a key from his pocket and pulled out a large black trunk from under the bed. He paused for a second and looked around at Precious who quickly slipped her dress to the floor. She wasn't wearing any panties. Maas Joe's eyes popped out of his head and he emitted a low moan as he looked at her naked form. He couldn't believe that this was happening to him. He fumbled with the lock for a few seconds before he finally managed to open it.

He pulled up the lid and opened it.

Precious was amazed. The rumor was true. The trunk was filled with stacks of money. Different denominations all neatly stacked.

Maas Joe smiled as he noted her reaction.

"See, mi 'ave money girl, nuh worry yuhself, Maas Joe will tek good care ah yuh."

Precious smiled and closed the lid to the trunk.

She pulled Maas Joe to her and pushed his mouth on her breasts. Maas Joe sucked them greedily as he caressed her body with his calloused hands. Precious sat down on the bed and spread her legs.

"Lick mi," she told Maas Joe.

Maas Joe sank to his knees quickly and buried his face in her pussy. It was dry but quickly became moist when she felt his gums on her vulva. Maas Joe had very little teeth and when he started sucking on her clit, Precious moaned like a wounded animal. The feeling of his tongue and gums was incredible. Her juices flowed like one of the many rivers running through St. Thomas. She grabbed his head and held it in place as Maas Joe sucked and sucked like his life depended on it. He was rewarded for his efforts five minutes later when Precious emitted a loud squeal as she shuddered and came violently in his mouth.

Slim Jim who was impatiently waiting around the corner by his donkey heard the scream and jumped. He tied the donkey to the fence and quickly made his way to the house.

"Open the window Maas Joe," Precious told him. The room had gotten really hot. Her pussy tingled as she watched Maas Joe hurry to do her bidding. He opened them and tied the curtains so that air flowed freely through the room. He ran back over to Precious and quickly dropped his pants.

She moved up on the bed as Maas Joe climbed on top of her anxiously. He grunted loudly when he penetrated her. In all his fifty years he had never experienced such bliss. He closed his eyes tightly as he savoured the feel of her sweet, succulent flesh.

"Lawd...Precious..." he moaned as he moved slowly inside her.

Precious, used to large dicks, did not feel a thing as Maas Joe stepped up the pace and started to stroke her furiously.

"Yes...Maas Joe...give it me..." Precious said, watching him as he struggled to delay his climax.

Slim Jim watched from the window in horror as he saw Maas Joe's bare, wrinkled ass going up and down as he pounded his wife to be. And she seemed to be enjoying it! He rushed around to the side door and tried the lock. It was open. The old man had been so excited he had uncharacteristically forgotten to lock the door. Slim Jim entered the house and charged into the bedroom.

Maas Joe was concentrating on his fast approaching orgasm and did not hear when Slim Jim entered the bedroom. Precious' mouth opened wide in surprise when she saw Slim Jim barge into the bedroom and grab Maas Joe by his ankles, pulling him unceremoniously to the floor.

"Rass!" Maas Joe exclaimed in surprise when he hit the hard floor with a thud.

Slim Jim rained blows all over Maas Joe's body, his eyes red with rage.

"Slim! Stop it!" Precious shouted as she jumped off the bed and tried to restrain him.

"Yuh sex him Precious! Yuh lie to mi!" Slim Jim lamented tearfully as he treated Maas Joe's prone body to a ferocious kick. Maas Joe grunted in pain and crawled out to the living room.

"Look Slim!" Precious said, lifting up the lid to the trunk. "Money fi wi!"

Slim's eyes widened as he looked at the stacks of money. "Mek wi kill him rass and tek de money and run way tonight Precious!"

"Tek who fah bloodclaat money?" Maas Joe declared from the doorway, holding his hunting rifle at the two conspirators.

"Shoot him Maas Joe!" Precious said quickly as she moved away from Slim Jim.

"Precious! Ah whey yuh ah do?" Slim Jim croaked in disbelief. He couldn't believe his love was double-crossing him.

"Shoot de bwoy Maas Joe! Yuh nuh see say him come fi rob and kill yuh?" Precious implored, holding one hand to her heart with a scared look on her face. "Rememba say mi ah yuh ooman now Maas Joe, and de teefin' bwoy come inna yuh house and disrespect yuh!"

"Yuh likkle traitor yuh," Slim Jim snarled and quickly rushed over to attack Precious.

She screamed as he grabbed her by the neck and proceeded to choke her.

"Let her go!" Maas Joe shouted as Precious struggled to break free from Slim Jim's grasp.

Maas Joe held the gun unsteadily as his hands trembled.

The gunshot was a loud boom after which there was an eerie stillness.

Maas Joe and Slim Jim froze in horror as they watched Precious' voluptuous body crumble in a heap on the floor.

"Jesus Christ!" Maas Joe said in a hoarse whisper.

Slim Jim sank to the floor and cradled Precious' head in his lap.

"Yuh kill mi Precious, oh Lawd gad, yuh kill mi Precious," he wailed in anguish.

OTHER TITLES BY THE AUTHOR:

Novels & Anthologies:
- ભ The Sex Files
- ભ The Stud
- ભ Merchants of Death: A Jamaican Saga of Drugs, Sex, Murder and Corruption
- ભ Erotic Jamaican Tales

Compilations:
LMH Official Dictionary Series (Co-authored with M. Henry):
- ભ LMH Official Dictionary of Caribbean Exotic Fruits
- ભ LMH Official Dictionary of Jamaican Religious Practices and Revival Cults
- ભ LMH Official Dictionary of Popular Jamaican Phrases
- ભ LMH Official Dictionary of Jamaican Words & Proverbs
- ભ LMH Official Dictionary of Jamaican Herbs & Medicinal Plants & their uses
- ભ LMH Official Dictionary of Jamaican History
- ભ LMH Official Dictionary of Sex Island Style
- ભ LMH Official Dictionary of Sex Island Style: Volume 2